apple and knife

**apple and knife** intan paramaditha

Harvill *Secker*
LONDON

Translated from the Indonesian
by Stephen J Epstein

1 3 5 7 9 10 8 6 4 2

Harvill Secker, an imprint of Vintage,
20 Vauxhall Bridge Road,
London SW1V 2SA

Harvill Secker is part of the Penguin Random House group of companies whose
addresses can be found at global.penguinrandomhouse.com

First published by Harvill Secker in 2018
First published by Brow Books in Australia in 2018

'The Blind Woman Without a Toe', 'Blood', 'Scream in a Bottle', 'The Queen',
'Vampire', 'The Well' and 'The Porcelain Doll' appeared in *Sihir Perempuan* by
Intan Paramaditha (Depok: Katakita 2005; reprinted with illustrations by
Gramedia Pustaka Utama, Jakarta, 2017).

'Doors', 'Beauty and the Seventh Dwarf', 'The Obsessive Twist' and 'Apple and Knife'
appeared in *Kumpulan Budak Setan* by Eka Kurniawan, Intan Paramaditha and Ugoran
Prasad (Jakarta: Gramedia Pustaka Utama, 2010).

The English translation of 'Apple and Knife' and 'One Firefly, A Thousand Rats'
appeared in *Spinner of Darkness and Other Tales* (Jakarta: Lontar/ BTW Books, 2015).

A CIP catalogue record for this book is available from the British Library

penguin.co.uk/vintage

ISBN 9781787301160

Publication of this book was made possible with assistance from the LitRI Translation
Funding Program of the National Book Committee and Ministry of Education and
Culture, the Republic of Indonesia.

Printed and bound in Great Britain by Clays Ltd, Elcograf S.p.A.

Penguin Random House is committed to a sustainable future for
our business, our readers and our planet. This book is made from
Forest Stewardship Council® certified paper.

contents

The Blind Woman Without a Toe

**Come. Come, child. Sit by me. Are you sure you want to hear** how I became blind? Oh, it's a scary tale, child. So much blood was shed, like when an animal is sacrificed. It was an awful event involving someone very close to me. You may know of her. I was butchered. Yes, you could say that. And I even butchered myself. My eyes were pecked out by a bird. They say it was a dove from heaven, but it was actually a black crow straight out of hell. I screamed. I begged it to stop. But my shrieks were drowned out by its caws. It got to the point that you could no longer tell what was flowing, tears or blood. The crow only heeded its owner and she wasn't satisfied until my eyes were hollow sockets.

Long ago, before I became blind, I lived with my mother and my two younger sisters. The youngest wasn't my biological sister. She was my stepfather's daughter. Her name was Sindelarat. You've heard of her, haven't you? She is already legendary, so maybe you won't believe what I'm about to tell you. Sin — that's what we called her — was so dirty, she looked like she had powdered herself with soot. And she really did live in the attic. I won't deny it (though I regret it, since that's where she colluded with the thing that granted her powers). What I want to do is correct history. History has killed me off in favour of her, who people say lived happily ever after. You want to know the real truth? Sin is dead. I'm the one who survives.

Yes, we were unfair to her. We ordered her to do the heavy work. When she wanted to go to the ball, we threw rice in every corner and wouldn't let her leave the house until she had gathered all of it in a bowl. Of course, it was wasted labour, but at that point we didn't know she was being helped by a spirit, that accursed Fairy Godmother. That's the story you've heard? Well, now I'll tell you something different.

Our stepfather loved Sin very much. Before he died, she was sweet and gentle and innocent — at least, that's how she presented herself. Father gave her beautiful dresses and a tiny tiara to sit atop her head of long gleaming hair. He admired his daughter's long eyelashes, especially when she fluttered them. Meanwhile, we were given Sin's old clothes. Good clothes, but hand-me-downs nonetheless. If he went on a trip, he would return home with a stack of presents for her, while my sister and I got a box of sweets. Our hearts burned with envy. How else could we have felt? A teenage girl's greatest accomplishment is owning piles of fancy clothes.

Father didn't scold or beat us, but he didn't accept us either. At dinner, the only one whose day he would ask about was Sin. How is your embroidering coming along? How are the roses you're tending? Is the chicken you're keeping laying eggs yet? What about the finch you're looking after, is its claw better? Has it healed?

The cake you made is delicious! Oh, look, Sin is so productive! Meanwhile, Father treated us almost as if we didn't exist, as if we were the remnants of a past that Mother had to lug around with her. His first wife had died and he needed someone to take care of him. He couldn't live without someone else's help. Someone to ready his breakfast, his clothes, his shoes. A companion to play around with under the mosquito netting. And he was crazy about Mother. She was a beautiful widow.

Mother was the flower of her village when she was young. Even though she was poor, all the men sought her hand in marriage. Back then only girls from rich families could go to school, so to make a living she worked as a maid in the home of a regent. Wanting to improve her station in life, she approached the regent after his wife died. Two months after that it was official: Mother became his wife. He was our biological father, though neither of us remembers him because he died when I was only two.

The people around us called Mother a harlot, saying she had used all the wiles at her disposal to get rich. Years later, they called my sister and me harlots too, when we were criticised for mistreating Sin. We got used to it, child. Our blood boiled like magma; we hated coming second.

For a dozen years, Mother lived off the wealth that our father had left behind. She was strong enough to care for us alone, but the estate of her deceased husband would only last so long. When I was fourteen, Sin's father, a close friend of my own father, grew close to Mother. People started gossiping about her anew. But once again, Mother didn't care. She married Sin's father shortly after his wife passed away. See, child, our family is used to making do with hand-me-downs.

Our stepfather of course could never be our biological father, but we wanted his attention too. We had learned that, in this world, fathers reign over everything. So, we hugged him and longed to climb on his shoulders and ride them as if we were riding power.

Sin, our stepsister, was an expert at putting on a sweet face. One day when my stepfather was about to go on a trip, he asked what gift we would like. Of course, because we rarely got nice presents from him, we said a beautiful dress. Sin said a rose would be enough. No wonder – even without Father travelling anywhere she got all sorts of extravagant treats. Notice how she wanted to play the part of a nice girl who isn't materialistic? Feh! Such a phoney. If she didn't care about money, then why did she insist on going to the ball to meet that filthy-rich Prince Charming?

Yes, that's how it was, child. Because we resented Sin, we made off with her beautiful dresses as soon as our stepfather died. We gave her our old clothes – which were her own clothes, gifted to us by her father, now returned to her once more. What was once yours is always yours, right? So began life without my stepfather.

Years passed. We grew into flowers ready to be plucked. But who did the young men sneak glances at in the market and the town square? That damned Sin. Even though she no longer had such beautiful clothes, her face was beautiful. Her skin had a golden glow. Her hair was black with lovely curls. She had a slender waist and shapely legs. Her voice was soft, appealing. We, on the other hand, had inherited more from our father than our beautiful mother: we were big-boned and dark-skinned. We could only gnaw our fingernails as the neighbours constantly remarked on how perfect she was. How upset we were when we learned that every last one of the young men lining up at the front door had come to seek Sin's hand! Mother tried to bargain, 'Sin is still very young. How about her older sisters marrying first?' But apparently that idea didn't appealed to anyone. Mother was angry and frightened that we might become old maids, so she sent Sin to hide in the attic whenever guests came. When in competition, women need to eliminate rivals and be unsparing in their hatred.

The ball was the climax of these events. We were merchandise in the market and Prince Charming was the sole customer. Of course, he couldn't purchase everything on display. He had to choose the best to be his queen. He could have a thousand mistresses if he desired, but there could be only one queen. We felt threatened by Sin's beauty that night so we did everything we could to prevent her from going. Sin whined that she wanted to attend, even though she had so many suitors already. Some were even sons of the rich! Why was she never satisfied?

As you well know, our efforts to discourage Sin that night failed because the Fairy Godmother considered her such a paragon of virtue that she waved her magic wand. Sin came to the ball. She was like a goddess sent from heaven and conquered Prince Charming by dancing flirtatiously with him. But the next day, news came that the prince had somehow lost his true princess. All that was left of her was a single slipper. The prince searched for the shoe's owner at every house, including ours.

Mother, still dreaming we could find a match of royal pedigree, made Sin hide when my sister and I took turns trying on the slipper. But the slipper was too small. I tried to force my foot inside. Alas, my toes were so bulky! My big toe was larger than most. Mother handed me a knife. 'Cut it off. You don't need it. If you become queen, you won't be doing much walking.' I took hold of the knife, bit my lip hard and amputated my toe. I tossed the first morsel of my flesh into the trash so that stray dogs could eat it. You would do well to know, child, that this world is filled with poorly fitting shoes that only accommodate the mutilated.

Once I had sliced off my big toe, I managed to squeeze into the slipper. I limped, grimacing. The slipper chaffed against the wound. Still, Prince Charming carried me off in his coach. I glanced at the dazed face of my future husband. He didn't look happy. He must have thought he had drunk too much the night before. How could the beautiful girl of his memories be me? He said nothing during the trip, until the chirps of a bird sounded:

> *Lo, behold this girl who lies*
> *Bloodying her slipper until it dries*

That bird – the crow from hell – pecked at the coach, desperate for its augury to be heeded. My husband-to-be ordered me to take off the slipper. He bellowed, almost fainting at the sight of my butchered flesh. He said nothing, asked me nothing. Without further ado, I was dispatched back home.

The tragedy was repeated. My younger sister was asked to try on the slipper, but her foot was too large as well. Only this time, her heel was what wouldn't fit. Like me, she carved off part of her foot with the kitchen knife. Like me, she stepped up into the coach and, down the road, was serenaded by the same snitch bird.

Prince Charming returned home, rage casting a shadow on his face. 'Don't you have another daughter?' he asked, furious at my mother for fobbing off rotten fruit. He wanted an unblemished apple. His viceroy ransacked our home, and found Sin in the attic. More precisely, Sin was waiting to be found; her sobs could be heard from outside. She was no less calculating than we were.

Yes, of course the slipper fit her foot; it was hers. Prince Charming lit up when Sin came down the stairs. He knew this was the woman from the ball. A woman who would make herself up every morning for him, who would anxiously await his return from the battlefield, who would bear his children. He immediately brought his beautiful princess home and they lived happily ev—

Wait, not yet. They didn't live happily ever after yet. Mother fell ill. She was depressed about my sister and me; we still hadn't found husbands. And butchering our feet had made our prospects even more dire. The townsmen looked away when we passed. Mother's illness worsened. She wrote to Sin but received no reply. Maybe Sin knew she wanted to borrow money. Finally, my sister and I went to see her in Prince Charming's magnificent palace. We arrived as she was enjoying her breakfast in a garden full of roses, jasmine, ylang-ylang and dahlias. The gurgling fountains were music to our ears.

Sin asked us to leave but we refused to do so until she gave us money. We also demanded to be mistresses to her husband, but of course thousands of beauties had already lined up for the position. Suddenly, that damned bird appeared, the same bird we had encountered on the road. It went after our eyes, stabbing at them with its beak, a knife weighted with vengeance. Again and again it stabbed. Sin, my stepsister, looked on. The last image I have of the world is the sight of her not lifting a finger to help, snacking on grapes.

Since then we have become the stuff of legend: Sin, the virtuous girl who wed, and we, the sisters, better off dead. We lived in poverty thereafter, supporting our ailing mother. She died with her eyes wide open. Until the end, she refused to accept the insults of those around her or the fact that we would forever be old maids. I left the village and now live as a wanderer with my sister. Two blind, useless women who survive by making music on street corners. My sister plays the harp and I sing. We must, for we have no Prince Charming, no Fairy Godmother.

Sin didn't live happily ever after. She died giving birth to her sixth daughter. Before that, she was pregnant almost every year because the kingdom needed a crown prince. Her thighs grew chubby and her stomach turned as flabby as bean curd. Excessive blood loss did her in, a fitting conclusion for this tale of gore.

Sin is dead. But, ah, who will listen to a blind, mutilated woman?

Blood

**On goes the light. The new LCD has just stopped projecting.** We're sitting around a table complete with laptops, BlackBerries, cell phones and half-finished coffee.

'These are the ads we made last year for Free Maxi Pads,' explains my boss, a woman in her thirties. 'We'll continue the series with the same theme. Menstruation as—'

Revenant. Monster.

'A very uncomfortable condition,' she says, then emphasises, '*without* Free Maxi Pads.'

She asks everyone to put forward an ad concept. Sort of a writing contest but with no prize money. The winner has the honour of developing the idea with a team, of leading a small group. There may even be potential for a promotion.

'Why don't you start by brainstorming. Let's get some thoughts on what a woman feels when she's having her period.'

'Cramps,' a copywriter responds.

'Pimples.'

'Good. But try to connect your ideas with our client's product.'

'Moist. Soaked. Smelly.'

'Dirty.'

'Nah!'

'Your turn, Mara.'

I think hard.

No, no, not now. Those were the words in my head when my first period came, during Ramadan. My mother had died giving birth to my sister the year before. Neither survived. All Mum left me were scraps of advice.

'Every woman will go through it, so you have to know how to use a sanitary napkin. It's not hard.' Mum demonstrated in front of me. I stood with knitted eyebrows, as if observing an alien's mucus. For me, it wasn't just the pad that looked strange but my mother's body, so unlike mine: full of grooves, streaks of white, veins of purple, hair like weeds. How many years before my body would fill with marks too?

'Don't look at me like that. It's no harder or stranger than tying shoelaces.'

I felt a budding pride. I'd been initiated into knowledge of what happens to a woman's body and how to handle it. I knew of important mysteries long before my friends.

But adulthood turned out to be closer than I imagined. It came when I was still too embarrassed to buy sanitary napkins at school, when I was in fifth grade. Other girls didn't get their first period until sixth grade, or even the second year of middle school. Why did my childhood have to end so soon?

After debating with the voices in my head, I settled on a small towel that I'd brought for gym class. A clever enough solution for the moment. May you feel proud in your grave, Mum.

'Well, Mara, your fast can never be one hundred per cent perfect again.' So said the ustadzah, my Qur'anic recitation teacher. We sat on my living room floor, the both of us pressing our thighs tightly together. She didn't like me to sit cross-legged.

'Why can't it be perfect?' I looked down. My words were more an expression of regret than a question.

I'd never managed to fast until six in the evening for thirty days straight. But now my fasting would be riddled with holes, like a grater, like an overused rag. I hated incompleteness.

After Mum died, Teacher came to our house often – so often that I thought Dad would replace the photo of Mum that hung on the family room wall with Teacher's picture. But two years later, Dad married again and I realised that Teacher would not be replacing my mother. I never got close to my stepmother but at least she didn't make up stories about how my mother went to heaven, in contrast to the wicked, who are tormented in hell. I didn't believe Teacher because once, before my mother died, she told me that heaven and hell were as dark as shadows. Sometimes heaven and hell perch on your head like a butterfly, she said, sometimes they disappear. Even though you are unaware that death is upon you, they appear to us in turn, as close as your breath.

When I told Dad about my period, he just commented awkwardly, 'Oh, I see.' Teacher's lecture came the next day. Dad and I were like a human and a wandering spirit. He needed a medium to reach me. Someone to act as a psychic. First Mum, then Teacher. He must have told her. Traitor.

'From this moment your sins are tallied, Mara,' said Teacher. 'Your mistakes are no longer your parents' responsibility but your own. So, bow your head at the sight of men. Have a sense of modesty. Don't speak loudly. You know, a woman should never become a singer.'

Wow. Mum liked to sing while she bathed. She fantasised about wearing a tight kebaya and performing with a gamelan orchestra, her hair tied in a knot.

'A woman's voice can tempt. It can invite fornication.'

'What's fornication?'

'What's between your thighs is a treasure. Don't sit with your legs open.'

'Why?'

'Many desire it. It is a source of disaster.'

'Why?'

Teacher never explained. I decided I wasn't allowed to know because each prohibition invited danger. If I understood, I would crave the forbidden. Menstruation led me to know of a treasure chest sealed tight. It needed to be buried away, hidden beneath the sea, because it was bloody.

'From now on you must rinse your pads and underwear,' said Teacher. 'Wash them so that they're spick and span, and then wrap them in newspaper.'

Why? Why? Why? Whywhywhy?

My teacher was getting exasperated at how I responded to each of her admonitions. She told me a strange story from her village about something that happened near the pesantren. One day, a girl was changing her napkin in a public restroom. She was in such a hurry that she forgot to rinse the pad and tossed it straight into the trash. When the girl got outside, it dawned on her that she'd left her ring behind. She ran back and opened the door to the toilet. Imagine her shock when she came upon a long-haired woman squatting, her back to her. When the woman turned, the girl saw her pale face and red lips and screamed. Even more horrifying, the woman was licking her blood-soaked pad.

Blood and ghosts, I nodded. It made sense. They always showed up together in stories. I stopped with my whys.

—

I need the right conditions.

I should be able to manage everything in the office, but I can't. In front of my computer, from nine to five, my job is to think up ideas. Yet not a single word or image comes to mind, not in the middle of all these computers constantly chirping out message alerts, not in my cramped rolling chair, with a limited set of positions to sit in, surrounded by colleagues in work shirts, sometimes joking, sometimes muttering who knows what. Ideas don't come to me here. They come in places that let my thoughts ramble and dance.

'You're a copywriter, you know, not a poet,' a friend said once.

'A copywriter isn't a photocopier.'

'What you are is a troublemaker. Don't tell me you have to get stoned each time you're after inspiration.'

No, I don't have to. Maybe what I need is to take a walk in the park, to feed the birds. Maybe I have to sit by a waterfall and watch water droplets flit about like flies. Maybe I have to get on a bus and make a survey of the city's smog through the window. Or become a fish — silent, motionless, mummified by time. And then when inspiration comes, I will dart at it.

But I'm a fish trapped in an aquarium. My gaze penetrates the glass, but keeps getting refracted in the process.

I need the right conditions. So, after work, I make an altar in my room. Laptop on a soft mattress. Dim reading lamp. Chill-out music. Strong black coffee, no sugar. A couple of slim joints. My holy shrine to the goddess of capitalism. I begin my quest for inspiration while chanting a mantra.

Oh, menstruation. Oh, menstruation. Ommm...

I always wear black trousers when I have my period. I was traumatised by the spots of blood that a friend noticed on the white skirt of my school uniform one Monday. I felt so ashamed. I was like Stephen King's Carrie at the senior prom, splattered and sticky with blood all over her face, chest, arms, legs. Hmm. How about borrowing that scene for my ad?

No, no. That would be repulsive.

Blood is fear. Madness. Women having periods can spread terror. But no one dependent on painkillers can be totally sane. And some of us are addicts.

My frustration grows. Has women's bleeding ever been the subject of poetry?

I think about tales of women in the harems of Istanbul. They were the most beautiful of women, handpicked by the sultan for his collection. Some were far more valuable than gold. After the first night, bloodstained sheets draped in the window would signal the sultan's pride at having lain with a pure maiden.

I twirl my pen round and round. My gaze wanders, follows the vertical and horizontal stripes on the ceiling.

I remember how my heart pounded when I was about to sleep with my first boyfriend. He and I were looking forward to it, including the blood. We were like little kids running around in anticipation of a rainbow after showering in the rain.

There was no blood.

'This isn't your first time.' His voice was soft but his words carried a rebuke. He turned around, his back to me.

It wasn't a question, so there was no need for me to respond.

Three days later, I seduced him in his car. He seemed to have developed amnesia about our recent Cold War skirmish. We parked on campus, behind a building that was rarely visited. He kissed me, his lips parched. This time he witnessed his coveted rainbow.

He jerked away, his fingers coated in blood.

I laugh. Uproariously. I, an adolescent. I, now alone in bed. I begin to drift, transported by the wild smoke. Anise, nutmeg, pepper and eucalyptus oil tickle my nose. Adolescent me and adult me are giggling, side by side.

'That's what you want, right?'

My beloved released me from his embrace, gaping. He stared at his palms, then looked at me in disgust. Blood soaked the back seat of his car, oozing into a pool of crimson. Menstrual blood.

After that act of revenge I promised myself not to shower in the rain with little boys.

And now I lose a lot of blood each month. My body smells of copper. Dogs sniff after me, follow along, their tongues hanging out.

Three years ago, being responsible about my sexual health, I asked a doctor what contraception suited me best.

An interrogation followed: 'Are you married?'

'No, I'm not,' I said.

Suddenly, he lost all interest in helping me. He began to lecture me while stealing glances at my breasts. The sight of his slick, bald pate made me feel strange. I had the urge to spew cockroaches all over him. I decided to go to another doctor, a woman with hair dyed auburn. She suggested an IUD.

She asked me to spread my legs wide. The chair I was in made me think of a seat in a rocket ship.

'The IUD is safe, but it'll mean more blood,' she cautioned. 'One pad may become two.' Two pads may become three. Three may become four. Four may become five. Etc., etc., etc., like the whining of pesky mosquitoes. The ceiling has begun to resemble a chequered tablecloth.

Shhh... Come on, focus.

Yes. Now I go through a pack of sanitary napkins in a day and a half. My body feels wrung out. What remains is my hollow womb, like a sponge that has been squeezed dry and then stabbed with a needle.

After the IUD was implanted my blood pressure fell dramatically. My head took a disliking to the rest of me. Every time I got up from a chair, it felt like rats were crawling over it, tugging my hair and nibbling my scalp. My body was shaky from carrying chubby little rats in my skull. I came to rely on tiny pills to boost the iron count in my blood. Red pills with a metallic smell. Deep red. Redder than the scar I'd seen on my mother's wrist.

(Mum, where are you? I'm lonely, I want to sleep next to you… I don't hear your voice anywhere, why did you come back after so many days with a scar on your wrist? Mum, Mum, don't be so quiet, talk to me – were you bitten by a wild animal, Mum? Have you become one of those who wander in the jungle?)

Hold on. Where did the rats go?

Weed always makes me drowsy.

———

I wake in the middle of the night, needing to use the bathroom. Eyes half-closed, I get out of bed. I open the door and walk through the living room. Things feel different. The television, the wardrobe, the desk, the chair and its cushions are gone. My house has narrowed to a hallway; both sides are lined by long, white benches. A hospital corridor.

I reach the end of the corridor. A door is ajar and I peek inside. There is a small table. Scissors. Cotton. Gloves. A light becomes ever brighter and more blinding. I spy a nurse holding my mother down, immobilising her. A man – a doctor, I think – is standing beside her open legs, straining. I can't see what is between those legs. Red. Blue. Watercolours blending into a thick clot. Blood of different colours and consistencies, strong tea, strawberry syrup, jelly. Mum is crying out. Her howls carry the pain of a lonely wolf.

A child stands by the edge of the door. She is in school uniform; her hair is short and she shoulders a small backpack.

(I'm here, Mum

here

HERE)

The girl is shouting in a vacuum.

'Who are you?' I ask stupidly.

Ah, no need. No need.

The girl is shocked to see the blood between her mother's legs. Blood flowing without cease, too powerful, too intense, murdering Mum. Is her sister emerging from the open rose petals?

A sister who doesn't cry. A sister who doesn't exist.

(Lucky you are, Sister, frozen for ever, inseparable from Mum, while I wander, my home lost)

My mother dies, making no effort to hold on.

(Mum Mum my tiny hand wipes my tears Mum I know you want to die you want to go but first tell me your secrets)

'Do you want to know about the red line on my wrist?' Suddenly, sweat on her forehead, Mum struggles into a sitting position and looks towards the girl.

The nurse and doctor also see her.

'It's blood,' the child says.

Mum shakes her head firmly.

'Blood is life,' she demurs. 'That line was my first death. I'm not dying here.'

The girl lurches like a startled horse.

I awake in my pitch-black room.

—

'Why?' My boss gapes like a goldfish, but her eyes smoulder like a hawk's. She wants to know the reason behind my resignation.

I say I've received another offer. That makes much more sense than saying that I can't be part of all this, sometimes present and sometimes not.

And it makes much more sense than to confess that I don't want to treat blood as an enemy.

I want drops of blood to be ink on my book, encrusted in the lines of destiny that twist and spin history on my palm. I want to make sacrifices like blood does, play with puddles, ooze sores, flare in anger.

My boss doesn't persuade me to stay, nor does she offer me a raise or promotion. She just nods and congratulates me. I don't know if I should be happy without the burden or take it as a slap in the face. I'm just a cog that can be replaced if it comes loose. They aren't losing me, and I'm not losing anything.

Once out of my boss's office, I head for the company toilet. Stress always makes me need to pee. Three doors, all marked blue instead of red. Blue means a stall is empty and red means it's not to be opened. Forbidden. I open the door at the end out of habit. I'm surprised, embarrassed: the stall is occupied.

'Sorry! I thought—'

I'm about to close the door again when something holds me back.

It's you.

You are that woman, hunched over, rummaging through the trash. Your hair is thick and stiff, dull, black broom bristles covering your face and shoulders. You're so comfortable there, like

30

the guardian of a shrine, keeping it as clean as can be, unclogging drains or groping to sweep dust and insects from under the bed.

I'm shocked.

You are the woman my recitation teacher told me about.

You turn around. I should be terrified, but I want to look at you. Your face is like paper in an old book, crumpled and pale. Dark circles frame eyes that protrude like marbles sprinkled with ash but, oddly enough, your lips are moist red, fresh. Beautiful.

'Why do you like blood so much?' I ask.

Your voice is hoarse and soft, so far away, so ancient. You whisper, 'Because it's life.'

**Bambang was found asphyxiated in his favourite car, a red** 1982 Mercedes Tiger. As if the fact of his death wasn't tragic enough, the state of his corpse was pitiful: he was reclining in his seat, naked, his safari suit crumpled beside him. Every part of his body lay exposed, subject to gravity's spite. The folds on his chin, his belly, his genitalia — everything appeared to sag, on the verge of collapse. Everything, that is, except his eyes. They gaped open, staring upwards in terror.

The condition of his body gave rise to several theories. Some doctors suspected he had masturbated himself into oblivion, not knowing that he had become trapped inside his car. The reddish marks on his neck were a puzzle, though. They seemed to indicate bites. Or, perhaps they came from a noose. Maybe Bambang had been seeing someone and that person had left him for dead in the car. But no fingerprints were found on the vehicle except his own. Then again, if this was a premeditated murder, the criminal wouldn't have been so stupid as to leave fingerprints.

Ratri, his wife, didn't cry. At the funeral, her face as she accepted the condolences of colleagues and relatives was so calm that it invited both sympathy and suspicion: what kind of woman could be so cool in the face of her husband's death? The unnatural demise made Bambang's corpse a spectacle, a mystery to be pursued in forensic labs, newspapers, and on television.

Inevitably, allegations emerged about Bambang's private life. Everyone knew that Bambang and Ratri had been sleeping in separate rooms. Surely a third party was involved. Perhaps Bambang had been finished off by a prostitute trying unsuccessfully to blackmail him, or a mistress fed up with his broken promises to marry her. Or perhaps his wife, who hadn't shed a tear, had hired a hitman.

Ratri made no attempt to stem the flow of gossip. After all, her husband was the director of a government agency. His case would be followed by a series of disclosures that would come one after the other, like toppling dominoes. Invisible hands, Ratri was sure, would turn off the tap. Which is exactly how it transpired. There was a national sense of crisis. But lurid fascination over the mingling of sex and politics was soon diverted to a parade of the usual problems. Ratri felt no need to share her secrets with anyone. She had predicted the tragic end would arrive soon enough. The Mercedes Tiger was cursed.

———

Several luxury cars were stored in Bambang's garage. For official occasions – trips to the office, inaugurations, weddings – Bambang drove his latest model Mercedes Benz. There was also a black Volvo. Its sleek elegance proclaimed Bambang's rank among high officials, ministers and even summit participants. But the

1982 Mercedes Tiger had a special status: it was Bambang's first car and was therefore historic. He treated it lovingly, only using it on special occasions. A toy imbued with nostalgia for youth. Bambang didn't let anyone else touch it, not even his chauffeur.

Six months earlier, a series of events had made Ratri think the car would no longer leave the garage. Bambang came home drenched in sweat after a drive. Their maid, Milah, discovered bloodstains on a tyre. Bambang had apparently hit a cat, something that had never happened in all the time Ratri had known her husband. Bambang always drove smoothly, was always in full control. Ratri didn't ask any questions because Bambang never explained anything to her.

After a while, Ratri started to have a bad feeling about the car. And, a few months before Bambang's death, she found her proof. She surreptitiously took the key from her husband's room when he was at the office and drove the vehicle to her boutique. Everything was fine until she pulled over and turned the motor off. She pressed the button on the key for the automatic lock. Click. The door was ready to be opened. However, unbidden, the four buttons dropped back down. Click. Click. Click. *Click*. It was as if a gang of invisible, rascally kids was teasing her. The doors locked again. Ratri pushed the button several times in vain. Panic set in. She looked out, hoping for a passing security guard. She looked to the right. To the left. In the rear-view mirror. She gasped. Someone was in the back seat.

—

Ratri and Bambang lived in a lavish, multi-storey residence with a spacious yard and high walls. A suburban castle. They moved there for a simple reason: such a palace was impossible in the city. A single road connected their neighbourhood to downtown. Jalan Baru, the new road and only access to the highway, was now being paved.

Behind one vacant parcel of land was a kampung. Rumours circulated that its residents would be evicted as mansions continued to be built. As far as tourist and development maps of Jakarta were concerned, the squatter settlement didn't exist. But the kampung had survived until now. Those within it bred, bartered and partied to the sounds of dangdut. Fearful of theft, the castle owners constructed imposing walls around their homes and installed barbed wire along them.

Since the death of their son, Anton, a few years before, Ratri spent more time at home. Anton had died in Los Angeles at the age of nineteen after crashing a motorcycle that had been a gift from his father. He was a sophomore at UCLA and had set out to explore Southern California. Once their son's body was brought home and buried Bambang and Ratri never discussed his death again.

After entering her forties, Ratri filled out a bit but remained attractive. She knew her husband's colleagues cast admiring glances at her, even tried to tempt her. But she had no interest in those pudgy men. She preferred to look after her home and oversee the running of her boutique a few times a week. She stayed faithful to her husband, who took to sleeping in a separate room after their son's death.

Bambang's vehicles conveyed a great deal about their relationship. Fifteen years earlier, Bambang would invite Ratri on drives out of the city in the Mercedes Tiger. Now he always left her behind. When the car left the garage, Ratri knew that Bambang wouldn't be home for several days.

At times Ratri suspected her husband was playing around with some model or starlet, as his colleagues did. But he mostly went to meetings with his subordinates and there were no women among them. And his secretary was a man in his mid-twenties who regularly visited their house for office business. Ratri concluded that her husband was a workaholic and that she had no competition.

The information Bambang shared with Ratri about his work went no further than what was reported in the media. Nonetheless, Ratri heard rumours of what was really going on. There were whisperings about a publicity-hungry young lawyer who had taken on an embezzlement case that would drag her husband down. Ratri understood that Bambang would fix the problem in classic fashion, as he had learned from his predecessors. A clean solution. Each access point clamped tight, like an iron gate. It was the era of the smiling general, when everything was always in order and violence left no mess. At first, the discovery of her husband's world horrified her, but Ratri learned to build her own walls. She prepared for the worst, secured her investments and arranged an emergency escape route for herself.

———

Feeling bored, Ratri opened the window. She saw Jamal, the new gardener from the kampung behind the vacant lots. He looked to be about the same age as Anton when he died. Jamal's strong and tanned arms gleamed as he planted rose seedlings. He was shirtless and in low-waisted trousers. Her eyes ran over the curve of his shoulder blades and the outline of his slim hips.

Less than two weeks after Jamal arrived, the door to Ratri's room lay open. Jamal appeared in front of her, his hands smeared in soil and his body smelling of the sun. Ratri beckoned him to close the door.

There were firsts for the both of them. Jamal had never touched a woman before. And Ratri had never had so many soil stains on her body.

———

Jamal was so obedient, so patient, so quick to learn. And not only in the garden. Ratri's feelings for him grew. She made him a household servant, gave him a room and raised his salary. Jamal accepted on the condition that he be allowed to go home to visit his mother on weekends. The young man lightened Milah's workload by sweeping and mopping every evening. He rose early in the morning to wash the car before Bambang left for work.

Between their lovemaking sessions, Ratri listened to Jamal talk about his life. In his kampung he had been known as a tourist guide of sorts. He often invited flocks of timid teenagers on excursions to look around. Outside the kampung he showed off his knowledge of who lived in the estates lining nearby Jalan Baru. This one belongs to a celebrity. A former minister lives over there. He called Ratri's home the 'the tax director's blue-walled mansion'.

Jamal gained broad insights from his connections. He befriended the security guards who popped outside the gates to smoke clove cigarettes together, and the maids who shopped in the local bazaar when their employers didn't visit the supermarket.

He'd had no intention of becoming a gardener. He wanted to be a driver. Until he started working for Bambang, he had supported his mother and younger siblings by driving a public minivan to and from Pasar Rebo. But he grew restless and harboured other dreams: to become a chauffeur for the owner of a Jalan Baru mansion. After becoming friendly with Mang Yayan, Ratri's guard, Jamal mustered the courage to ask about the possibility of working in the house.

Unfortunately, said Mang Yayan, Mr Bambang was not looking for a chauffeur. Besides, the one who worked for him had years of experience. But Mr Bambang was looking for a gardener.

Ratri asked, 'How long have you wanted to be a chauffeur?'

Jamal blushed, arousing Ratri's passion. The answer to her question was postponed.

———

Bambang was the last in the house to learn that Jamal had become Ratri's personal assistant. That night, he had just come home from the office when he ran into Jamal as the youth was leaving Ratri's room. Jamal bowed in fear, not daring to meet the searching gaze of the master of the house. Ratri appeared behind him and challenged Bambang's look. She said, 'Jamal gives wonderful massages.'

Ratri thought Bambang would fly into a rage and hurl Jamal out, not from jealousy, but to assert control over his territory. She was wrong. Bambang said nothing and continued on to his room, leaving Ratri with the still-shaking Jamal. Her husband was overly close-mouthed, perhaps because she was not as valuable to him as the Mercedes Tiger. It was also possible that Bambang had concocted a plan that she could not hope to guess at.

The next day, Bambang came home early. Through the crack of her bedroom door, Ratri saw that the door of Bambang's room was open. He was wearing a black silk kimono that made his sagging belly more prominent. Not long after, Jamal appeared at the stairs.

'Let's see how good at massage you really are,' he said to the boy in a husky tone.

Jamal vanished within and the door closed.

Jamal wasn't fired. But things changed after that night. Jamal's mind seemed elsewhere when he made love to Ratri.

'What is it?' asked Ratri. 'Do you have a girlfriend in your kampung now?'

She regretted fitting him out with new clothes that would have made him more handsome in the eyes of the kampung girls. But something else seemed to be afoot. He still visited her but only touched her robotically. He no longer told her about himself. Instead, he hid his thoughts from her. And then, one day, Jamal faced Ratri, his eyes full of trepidation. He told her he could no longer be her special assistant.

Ratri let the boy stay on to work in the house – sweeping, mopping, washing Bambang's car. And every night, Jamal climbed the stairs and slipped into a bedroom to offer a massage. Not Ratri's room, but Bambang's. He would not leave until the following morning.

———

Ratri was no longer sure what Jamal was to her: gardener, slaker of lust or simply a young man the same age as Anton? She had lost a great deal: the pleasure of presenting new clothes to him, preparing special meals for him and, most of all, soaping his back whenever the two of them soaked in the bathtub together. Ratri remembered how eagerly she would listen to his tales.

'You still haven't answered my question,' said Ratri as her fingers glided over his skin. She reminded him that she had asked, once, why he wanted to become a chauffeur.

Jamal was slow to begin. It all started one day when he was washing behind his house. His thoughts drifted. The enclosure surrounding the bath was made of plywood and was a mere inch taller than he was. The babble of kids playing marbles nearby floated over it. A guava tree beyond the enclosure was fruiting. He caught sight of someone – another village youth, Hamid by name. Jamal's body was still slick with soap when their eyes met. Hamid clumsily scrambled down the tree. Taking his time, Jamal covered his body with a towel. Then he went over and confronted Hamid. Afterwards, he returned to the bath enclosure, still soapy, wondering whether Hamid had ever peeped at his mother and sisters.

Jamal mused that a plywood door was very different from the high metal gates of the houses along Jalan Baru.

'You can't spy through those gates,' he said.

'And who would you want to spy on?' teased Ratri.

Jamal confessed that from that point forward he often wondered what life was like behind the gates, and fantasised about making a life on the other side of them. Fancy cars came and went, arousing his curiosity about driving one. He didn't care to be the owner, he just wanted to try one out. He imagined gripping the steering wheel in the air-conditioned enclosure. He would stare at the scorched, dusty city from behind the tinted windows. Behind them, he would be invisible, an undetected voyeur.

'Oh, you clearly were born to be a tour guide.'

'It's not just the rich who like being tourists,' Jamal said.

Ratri finally understood what happened to Jamal when Bambang's vehicle left the garage early one morning. He wasn't driving the late model Mercedes Benz but rather the historic 1982 red Tiger that was off-limits to Ratri. And in that car sat Jamal. He had found another door.

Jamal returned the next day, beaming. Ratri found him in his small room and he hurried to rise from the mattress. He looked like he was steeling himself for a scolding. His expression quickly turned to surprise when Ratri spoke.

'You need to remember one tourist tip: no matter what happens, never fall in love.'

Ratri's warning came too late.

She wasn't sure if Jamal understood, but at least the advice let him know that she didn't hate him. On another occasion, he approached her. He hesitated and then hugged her close. He whispered a secret in her ear. In response, she stroked his hair slowly. She never told his secret to anyone.

In the vehicle, Jamal's skin rubbed against the cool seat. And he felt a soft but firm touch all over. The touch of an experienced driver in full control, in an enclosed space, hidden by the gleaming doors, the tinted glass.

———

After passing through Ratri's house gates, Jamal made his way through a series of doors. But his life really changed after the door of the Mercedes Tiger opened.

Compliant with her husband's wishes, Ratri continued to accompany Bambang to weddings. She obeyed unwritten rules in front of officials' wives, fulfilling her obligations, invoking Bambang's name. Oh, he's so busy lately. Last week he was out of town, inaugurating something or other.

But, except for official ceremonies, it was now Jamal who stood at Bambang's side. He no longer wore the sweatshirt and jeans that Ratri gave him, but black trousers, a shirt and a black leather jacket that made him look older than his years. Now he smoked Lucky Strikes and used a Zippo lighter bearing a Los Angeles Lakers logo, which Bambang had bought while visiting Anton. Jamal appeared to be doing important work for Bambang, but at home he still happily lathered his boss's beloved Tiger, polishing it until it sparkled, caressing its smooth doors.

Ratri couldn't say for certain what Jamal did away from the house. She also didn't know which had ensnared Jamal more: Bambang, or a door opened just for him. But she smelled danger. She was anxious when he came home late. Jamal pooh-poohed her concerns, drunk on love.

'So, you've become one of his thugs, huh?'

Jamal looked dazed by Ratri's interrogation. He sighed and then, with a far-off expression, said slowly, 'Mr Bambang drives so smoothly. You should see how he handles the steering wheel, takes charge of the gears.'

The danger that Ratri had sniffed from the beginning became concrete one sunshiny morning. Ratri called Jamal to her room. Unusually, she let him see her with her hair in disarray. Her eyes were swollen. She tossed the morning paper towards Jamal.

Headlines on the front page blared out the death of a young solicitor. The publicity-hungry lawyer had been found dead in his car, stabbed seven times. Police suspected that several people had been in on the murder. One of them had rashly left behind a Zippo lighter with a Los Angeles Lakers emblem.

'Really, really stupid,' Ratri muttered.

For some time, Jamal remained frozen. Ratri refused to ask him why – his love for Bambang, or for doors. Both were now equally nauseating. Jamal had become a fugitive. And Bambang despised carelessness.

Jamal couldn't stay there. Ratri asked him to leave.

'But Mr Bambang loves me,' Jamal protested. It was clear he didn't want to leave the house, not through any door.

'Bullshit,' snorted Ratri. She jerked Jamal's hand, pulling him out of the room. Her knees were shaking as she went down the stairs beside him. She emptied his wardrobe and packed his clothes.

'Get as far away as possible,' she said. 'Don't go to your mother's. And don't even think of coming back here.' Then she slammed the door.

---

The night was dark. Ratri was driving the red Mercedes Tiger along a winding road lined with stately trees. There was no light apart from the car's headlights. There were no signposts. Ratri caught something out of the corner of her eye. A figure running along the side of the road. She wasn't sure who he was. Ratri stopped and backed up. But she couldn't see him any more. She was alone on an endless, winding road.

For three days after Jamal's departure, nightmares interrupted Ratri's sleep. Recurrent dreams about a car and a mysterious figure that disappeared on the road.

---

Ratri had told Jamal not to contact her. Even so, she camped in the living room in case the phone rang. Secretly, she hoped he would let her know he was okay.

The fourth day after Jamal left, the phone rang at eleven at night. The call wasn't for her. The phone was connected to the master bedroom, and Bambang had already picked it up.

'Hello?'

'Sir.' The sound of panting. 'They're after me.'

'Where are you?'

'Help me.'

'Stay there. I'll come and get you. Where are you?'

Ten minutes later, Bambang emerged from his room, look-ing purposeful. He was dressed sharply. Another man trailed Bambang, smoothing his clothes. His secretary.

Ratri stood, tensed, at the end of the stairs.

'I'm coming with you.' Her voice was soft but determined.

Paying no heed to the secretary, Ratri hastened her step and followed her husband to the garage. They had no time to argue because, as soon as the car door opened, Ratri nimbly made her way into the passenger seat. Bambang turned to her. There was no anger in his eyes. Ratri felt that he was deliberately allowing her in.

Bambang pressed the automatic lock. They drove, not passing through the toll gate towards the city, but continuing along Jalan Baru in the other direction, to wherever it was that it stopped. Ratri had never been this way, but it wasn't unfamiliar. Her night-mares. The same deserted road. Darkness. No lights. No signs.

Bambang parked the Mercedes Tiger on the side of the road without turning the motor off. Being with her husband in a con-fined space, not speaking to each other, Ratri felt jittery, but the sound of the engine and air-conditioning rescued her.

In the distance, someone emerged from the bushes, running towards the Mercedes Tiger. In Ratri's dreams, the figure was blurry. Now she saw it was Jamal. He was wearing the same black trousers and jacket and looked exhausted.

Suddenly, two men appeared from behind the trees and chased after him. Jamal reached the vehicle and pounded on the door, shout-ing for Bambang. The men caught up to Jamal and grabbed him. One of them had a rope in his hand. He looped it around Jamal's neck.

'Open the door!' Ratri screamed.

Her husband stared straight ahead. Bambang must have had it all planned. In total control, like the way he drove.

When she thought back on the incident, Ratri couldn't remember how long Jamal struggled. She had reached for the lock but Bambang seized her wrist. Her hands were weak. Jamal flailed at the door. He continued to stare inside and his mouth moved, as if he were saying something. The glass began to fog up. Ratri was still trying to make out what he had said when she realised that she was staring at the wide eyes of a corpse.

Jamal's body slumped against the car. A final door that did not open for him.

———

Ten years after Bambang's death, Ratri sat behind the wheel of the Mercedes Tiger. She was now fifty-two years old. Beside her sat a young man. An activist, or so he said, although for Ratri he remained an enigma. Activist, slaker of lust or simply a young man the same age as Anton? They talked for a long time about the election and the return to candidacy of so many of the same old faces. 'How funny,' said Ratri. 'So much had been forgotten in ten years.'

'Yes,' said the activist, yawning. 'By the way, why don't you sell this car? It gives me the creeps.'

'Why?'

'Why? It's where your husband died. Sometimes I feel like I'm being watched.'

'Do you remember how he died?'

The man relayed what was reported in the media. 'Anyway, your husband was an important man,' he said, trying not to offend Ratri with the mention of corruption. Ratri smiled. She nurtured a different memory, of something unheard, considered unimportant.

On the day Bambang died, she got the answer: not to the riddle of her husband's death, but to a question of her own. She had wondered whether Jamal's story had truly ended there. Indeed, she didn't care why or how Bambang died. That day she knew that a message was sent, though it was not easy to decode. Maybe the ghost of Jamal was taking vengeance over unrequited love and the betrayal of his trust. But even the motive of revenge couldn't explain away Jamal, a young man obsessed by doors, a young man who would force entry and refuse to budge.

Ratri pulled the car over. She dropped the activist off in front of his house. He gave her a peck on the cheek before getting out.

Ratri stepped on the gas and stared at the figure in the rear-view mirror, laughing.

**After that evening, Kuchuk Hanem – let's call her that, as few** knew her by her real name – would linger in the men's memories even after they returned to their continent. Her two guests were indistinguishable from other tourists, their whiteness and curiosity making them easy targets for thieves. They had come expressly to see her, the most famous courtesan in Esna. She stood at the top of her spiral staircase, her chin raised, inspecting her prey with imperious eyes. The strands of her necklaces glistened. Kuchuk Hanem let the pair gawk at what they could make out of her body beneath her gauzy lavender robe. Her mastery of the pose allowed her to evoke divinity. She had ordered her servant, accompanied by a ewe coloured with henna, to escort the gentlemen to her residence.

Only later did Kuchuk Hanem find out that her visitors, a photographer and a writer, were distinguished in their land of archivists. The former was obsessed with ruins and geometry; the latter, with the human or, rather, the half-human. The writer, while never losing respect for his photographer friend's obsession with visual fidelity, indulged his own passion for the world around him by describing his encounters with hybrid creatures that were part goddess, part animal, part devil. Despite their different natures, the pair had sailed up the Nile to record this antique land, the playground where Kuchuk Hanem had learned to perform – and cheat – in her games. They had equipped themselves with a map inscribed with the respectable mission of bringing back knowledge about this other world. Through their eyes, one might see the curves of Kuchuk Hanem's body haunting the severe lines of pyramids, and all Egypt incarnated in her kohl, in her henna, in the rattles on her anklets, in the beads of sweat on her décolletage.

—

Maxime Du Camp and Gustave Flaubert sat on a divan puffing pipes as Kuchuk Hanem, three dancing girls and a small band of musicians prepared for the show. Kuchuk Hanem had washed the guests' hands with rose water. Ah, these khawajah loved rituals – the more bizarre the better, and the more profitable for the performers. Gustave didn't have high expectations. His brief experience of Egypt's demimonde gave him the impression that the beautiful women here danced terribly. The most thrilling dance he had witnessed was performed by a male. Hasan el-Belbeissi, he wrote, wore wide trousers that allowed one to glimpse the slope of his naked buttocks.

The dancing girls could never compete with Hasan's pelvic gyrations but they were 'learned women' nevertheless. 'The equivalent of our intellectual Parisian ladies,' Gustave whispered in Maxime's ear.

Awalim, or 'learned women', meant prostitutes.

The Dance of the Bee was the evening's highlight. The musicians lowered a fold of their turbans to cover their eyes. Only Gustave and Maxime would have the honour of witnessing the special dance in that cramped, dimly lit space. One rabab player was reluctant to blindfold himself and, for reasons unfathomable to the French travellers, fixed them with a hostile stare. The man appeared old and haggard. He had a skeletal figure and long, bony fingers. His face was dark and he had sunken cheeks and a thin moustache.

'Mehmet,' Kuchuk Hanem called his name gently and winked.

Gustave and Maxime guessed that this Mehmet was protesting. His broken voice was indistinct. For Gustave, such unintelligibility went beyond a language barrier. He couldn't tell whether the man was uttering a sentence, presumably unfinished, or was simply grunting like a pig. His tongue seemed trapped. Gustave could only hear choppy laryngeal sounds, conjuring images of a rite to resurrect the dead.

'No need for him to close his eyes if he doesn't want to. The old man is quite harmless,' said Maxime, who had little interest in local dramas.

Confronted with Kuchuk Hanem's stubbornness over the integrity of her performance, Mehmet finally gave up. But the phrase 'gave up' didn't reflect what was in his eyes just before he applied the blindfold. Something was festering there, decaying slowly, as if Mehmet himself had started decomposing long ago.

In the next moment, Kuchuk Hanem transformed into a beautiful girl pondering a lover, motionless, her feet fixed on the ground. Suddenly, a shrill. The music grew frantic, terrifying, like an angry bee. Such a merciless bee it was, darting at her breasts, making her writhe, her feet still grounded, compelling her to shed all her garments. As she jerked her hips in a frenzy, Gustave observed the folds of flesh on her belly and caught a faint scent of turpentine emanating from her skin. Perhaps not Hasan el-Belbeissi, Gustave thought, but a muse regardless.

The Bee was hardly the Muse's favourite piece of choreography, but at least it allowed the pleasure of acting silly rather than sexy.

———

When the musicians left at eleven, the air was still heavy with perfume, perspiration and smoke. The travellers decided to spend the night. Gustave noted that Maxime appeared exhausted and concluded that this could not be due merely to the intense revelry of the past four hours (with the occasional interlude for a bout of fucking, he added in an arch note). The photographer, who possessed an admirable, perhaps self-destructive, desire for precision, may have been contemplating the balance between light and shadow in his images, or whether the calotype would convey the perfection in scale and detail he had envisaged. Maxime always remained fully absorbed in his project — a raging mania for photography, Gustave called it — even while amusing himself with a whore or two. Kuchuk Hanem, who couldn't bear to see a man unmoved by her charms, teased Maxime. 'Would you like to take pictures of me while you're here?'

'Apologies, Mademoiselle. I only photograph historical monuments. Ours is a mission in the service of science.' His tone was polite and distant, though he had already surveyed her legs and torso, appraised her proportions.

'As you wish. Besides, I'm not the best at sitting still and keeping my mouth shut,' she laughed coyly. She was a poor actress when she pretended to be humble. Maxime looked away and forced a cough.

Gustave went to Kuchuk Hanem's bedroom while Maxime slept alone on the divan. Later that night, on her palm-branch bed, Kuchuk Hanem already found herself unable to recall whether she'd had an orgasm. To be fair, Gustave's member entertained her well enough. Ditto his tongue. He was a perfectionist in matters of arithmetic; he took notes. Five times (he counted his coups, mon ami, not hers). The third was the most ferocious. The writer catalogued his virility in letters to his dear friend Louis Bouilhet.

After they made love, Gustave wiped his semen with a handker-chief and proffered it to Kuchuk Hanem. She raised her eyebrows.

'My mistress in Paris treasured evidence of our heated coup-lings,' he said.

In fact, Gustave was referring not to his mistress but to Maxime's. In recalling his tumultuous affair with the poetess Louise Colet, he delighted in imagining her as a woman who archived all that was ephemeral, including his ejaculations. In return, she had given him a lock of hair from the deceased Chateaubriand, her literary hero.

Kuchuk Hanem demurred, little impressed by the notion of immortalising bodily fluids (a week later, she cursed Gustave, who had deposited a different sort of keepsake with her: syph-ilis). Gustave was disappointed that his passion for metaphor went unrequited. Louise would have behaved otherwise, he thought, for she was a writer who read poems composed in an elegant tongue and had translated Shakespeare; she was a creature with a capacity for abstract thought.

Perhaps Kuchuk Hanem required a more straightforward thank you. Gustave gave her a wooden doll he had purchased in a nearby market. She smiled and pecked him lightly on the cheek, as if thanking a good boy. Gustave persisted: 'In exchange, may I have that beautiful item?' He gestured at the long golden shawl she had worn during the dance, now discarded on the floor. He bent down to stroke the delicate fabric, imagining how, many years after Esna, it would speak to him of the irretrievable: this room, this air, this corporeal Muse.

It is an old custom, unthreatening for many. Travellers leave traces where they visit and take something home in return. Without souvenirs, the verity of a travel narrative is called into question.

Yet it was a logic of transaction that she refused to adopt.

'Then may I ask you to sell it to me?' Gustave cajoled her.

She said no once more, this time more firmly. She was perched on one side of her bed, arms folded and legs unmoving.

Lying beside Kuchuk Hanem, Gustave replayed his memories of nights of worship in Paris. He remembered brothels, faint lamplight, women in low-cut dresses sauntering in the rain. Like any true artist contemplating encounters with whores, Gustave set himself adrift in melancholia. He mused on the ascetic façade that denied carnal pleasure, the mystique of the transient and the profane, et patati et patata. Prostitutes are poetry. Kuchuk Hanem snored loudly.

Gustave and Maxime set out the next morning. A new adventure called. Off to a hunt! Gustave scratched at his back. Kuchuk Hanem's bedbugs were especially ill-mannered towards foreigners.

By the time his state-sponsored trip to the Orient came to an end, Gustave had gathered all manner of curios. A cornucopia of costumery, gazelle and lizard skins, a small embalmed crocodile from Nubia, hashish from Cairo, silks from Beirut, rosaries from Jerusalem. Maxime, whose interests lay only in the antique and the dead, consoled him: Kuchuk Hanem's shawl was nothing special. Yet Gustave couldn't dismiss it so easily, not even when he had reconciled with Louise and his friendship with Maxime had soured. But he also took solace in images and feelings he had recorded in his mind, in all that his senses witnessed. There is no finer archivist than a European man of letters.

———

Kuchuk Hanem sunk into bathwater scattered with flower petals, and afterward reclined on her bed. Mehmet, the aged rabab player, appeared in the doorway. He was a faithful lover, as devoted as a dog. For the past decade, he had gone wherever Kuchuk Hanem led, from the bustle of cosmopolitan Cairo to the village of Esna, where she and other dancing girls, courtesans, and other Egyptians of dubious cultural pedigree had been exiled. Her unruly body may have disgraced the modern Pasha, but not Mehmet.

Mehmet walked silently to the bed. He showered his lover's feet with kisses. Kuchuk Hanem felt something wet her toes. His tears.

'What is it, my love?'

He didn't answer. His face sank between her thighs. She closed her eyes, ran her fingers through his grey hair. Sometimes she thought she truly loved Mehmet. She felt an enormous contentment in acting as a generous mistress who showed compassion towards her slave. His face was ugly and his mouth too big. Any comparison with her young admirers – such as handsome Monsieur Flaubert, before he went bald – would be cruel. Yet, she would never trade Mehmet's tongue for the tongue of any of her white lovers. His was not a tongue that took possession of the earth, but a tongue so gentle as to thrill the bones. She moaned.

An Oriental woman is but a machine, wrote Gustave, to assuage the fury of Louise.

It never occurred to Kuchuk Hanem to ask Mehmet if he'd known jealousy. Sentimentality was his fate; it had no place on her stage.

Mehmet was so slight that the voluptuousness of her body overwhelmed him. He submitted to her orders, stroking here, nibbling there, faster, harder, all to worship the great Kuchuk Hanem. How she adored bearing witness to his wild desire for her, fierce and ravenous, and hearing his words of veneration in her ears, from the amorous to the obscene. Yet that day, towards the end of their violent lovemaking, his energy subsided gradually. His increasing lassitude was almost imperceptible. Faintly, she heard him making a desperate hiss, like a wounded animal.

The sun had almost set when Kuchuk Hanem awoke to find herself alone. Mehmet wasn't by her side. She called out to her cherished slave but received no reply. As she rose to her elbows, something caught her eye. She screamed. Her soft skin was splattered with blood. Something cold and moist lay on her stomach.

———

Mehmet never returned. On Kuchuk Hanem's small dining table was a letter and a knife stained with dried blood, pointing at her.

*My love,*
*I see the future. So clear, just as when I saw you dancing*
*last night, even though my eyes were shut. You will see*
*it too, one day. I cut off my tongue with my own hands*
*before another cuts it off for me. I could envision them*
*silencing me slowly, muting me — those who travel far,*
*those who peer through cameras.*
*Remember me always.*

Kuchuk Hanem crumpled the letter, cursing her romantic, foolish lover, cursing his nonsensical prophecy. In anguish, she hurled her antique lamp against the wall.

She painted her eyes and smiled coy greetings at market-goers. But in the evenings, she cried for hours in her bath. On the fifth day after Mehmet left, she was so weak she couldn't leave her bed. (It was unclear whether her infirmity was caused by the loss of her devoted slave or by syphilis.) In the throes of her high fever, she thought of many things – of how she would have posed if Maxime had agreed to photograph her; of what Gustave would say to the Parisians about her bedbugs; of how Gustave's mistress would react to tales of her hips; of who would look at their photographs and read their accounts; of eloquent tongues; of a mute rabab player. This was no delirium. Everything was lucid. Then, one dry night, she decided to end her mourning. She had an idea about keepsakes, one that her jealous lover could never have imagined.

For the next decade, every time a foreigner expressed his desire for her shawl as a souvenir, Kuchuk Hanem would refuse.

'Then what can I give you for it?' the visitor would ask.

She would give an enigmatic smile and say, 'I don't confuse my heart and my cunt.'

Thinking she was demanding an exorbitant price, the gentleman would mention an amount of money. She would respond with a little laugh. Then, she would rise from the bed and, with that serpentine sway of her hips, she would stride to the cupboard in the corner of the room and return with a bottle of murky liquid.

'Long ago, I gave my shawl to a man from Cairo named Mehmet. In return, he gave me this souvenir.'

In the bottle, the visitor would behold not a genie, but something altogether less mystical.

The sight was so repulsive and humiliating that it silenced them. None of those who came later – tourists, archaeologists, writers, politicians – recorded this event. Because Kuchuk Hanem's souvenir, unlike a sweat-stained shawl or an embalmed crocodile, mocked them. Because it held up a mirror, and that mirror revealed a hideous face. Because it revived the memories of a thousand other tongues they didn't comprehend, of guttural sounds from the back of the throat, savage and mischievous. And a language as beautiful as the devil's had no place in this world. Such a language was meant to dissolve with the sound of the desert wind, to be buried with the ruins of ancient tyrants.

In Maxime Du Camp's photographs of statues, pyramids and temples, a dark figure is often visible, a small and lovely ornament, like a tattoo inked onto the colossal shoulder of Ramses. Had those figures ever made a sound?

Scream in a Bottle

'What's a nice girl like you doing in a place like this?'

Gita sees the woman for the first time. Her face is hard, cheekbones high, jaw sharp. Her sallow, mottled skin does little more than mask her wispy frame. Cheap batik is draped haphazardly around her waist, and a black kebaya and black headscarf render her even more sombre. As soon as she draws near, Gita catches an odd, pungent odour. It's not human sweat but fragrant cloves from a distant realm, incense for departed souls, stiff bodies bathed in flowers before being placed into the grave.

No scent of life wafts from the abode. Its distance from the city and its seclusion should have freshened the house but the owner cares little for ventilation. Brown curtains dangle in the windows. Branches of frangipani shade the yard, making the sun reluctant to greet the weeds spreading on the ground. A dark fence, peeling and rusty, serves as a barrier between the house and the outside world.

Like a snail in a shell, shunning interaction.

And rightly so. The woman now in front of Gita is notorious in her hometown, which is nestled up against the cliffs of Cadas Pangeran. People speak of her only in whispers. Sumarni. A witch. A sorceress allied with the devil. A second Mak Lampir, the evil conjurer. Yes, Lord, she will burn in hell until the strips of her flesh sizzle. Yes, Lord, may she not find forgiveness.

Gita realises that the woman is waiting for her to answer.

'I'm doing research,' says Gita, trying to conceal her nervousness, and to convey an attitude of respect. 'Of course, your name and place of residence will be disguised.'

The wrinkled woman squints and regards her coldly: 'That is necessary.'

Her eyes probe, trying to confirm that Gita hasn't smuggled in a camera or some other recording device. Maybe the woman has lost a substantial sum buying off the police. Or maybe she is irritated because most visitors take advantage of her. Recently, a TV crew came from Jakarta to interview her as a source for a crime drama. They broadcast her later in blurred black and white, masking her eyes with a thick strip. The episode's title? 'The Dark Side of Women.'

Gita enquires delicately about the woman's profession. What it is that she does. How long she has been... practising it.

Embarrassed, Gita dares not utter the phrase that dances in her thoughts: disposing of life. It sounds like a mantra of the damned.

The old woman's lips are clamped shut, even though she has already worked out the situation. She knows what people expect of her. The mark is on her forehead, a bright red stamp that will never disappear.

'I've been doing this a long time,' she says, slowly and heavily. 'Maybe thirty years. Maybe more.'

It's as if time is gnawed away by termites here. The hours melt into the night, and the tick of the clock no longer matters.

'Why do they do it?'

'They don't want to, child, but nature punishes those who give in to lust. They can't control themselves: their eyes, their fingers, their breath, their womb. They are like leaves that yellow, dry up, and fall to the ground.'

'I don't understand.'

'Ah, no one tries to understand.'

'Why do *you* do it?'

Sumarni's lips turn up slightly at the corners. She seems almost to smile, but no smile is reflected in her grey eyes. Gita watches as those eyes become the sky. Clouds gather within; they let loose rain, but no thunder.

'Child, for the sake of one life, sometimes you have to extinguish another. Some birds must destroy themselves in flame to give birth to a new generation. We consider it natural, even noble, to be born to sacrifice. Like Sinta in the Ramayana. And therein lies your value. You never knew, child, that dead birds surround you, breathing the same air as you. They look alive, but maggots, invisible to the eye, gnaw their rotting flesh. They are only present as givers of life; like water, sometimes polluted, which gushes forth continuously formless. Water can only mould itself to the vessel.

'And I, child, I have indeed been an ally of the devil. Because I know that some birds don't want to destroy themselves in flames. I know that there are waters that simply want to freeze rather than become wellsprings for the sake of a stillness that they have never known.'

Rain falls in the yard, soaking into the earth. Not a downpour, but slow, drop by drop. A long, soft tone, like a bow sliding against a violin string. Gita feels a chill. Fog is on its way.

'So, the lewd seek your services.'

'Those fine fingers of yours, child, were not made to point in accusation. It is not only the lewd. A mother of four came to see me. A woman you wouldn't suspect, a nice girl, like you. She was no tourist at the beach, but a wanderer in the desert. She had grown hunchbacked from carrying too many heavy loads. She needed to do what she did to remain strong and accompany her master, who had to find a means of subsistence until they reached their destination.'

'What do you require?'

'Money, of course. I need to live, my dear. Then fabric for a sling. So that the baby can feel the mother's embrace in the world beyond. The fabric can serve as a link if the soul of the baby longs for its mother or the mother longs for the baby. A bridge of sorts. But sometimes, the bridge is cut off. Sometimes, the mother goes crazy. The baby becomes an angel. They don't need to know each other.'

'But why?'

'You're repeating the question, child. Mothers can't just bundle up their babies and toss them into the trash as easily as acrobats do tricks. Their determination is not like the roar of a beast. It is like the footsteps of soldiers who march onward, well aware that they are marching to their doom.'

Gita feels another chill. Suddenly, she hears those footsteps, growing ever clearer, racing as bombs explode in the distance. Dust and grit mingle and obscure her vision, bringing blinding pain.

'There are tears in your eyes,' says the old woman. 'Maybe slivers of glass got in. War destroys everything.'

'And then?'

'Then, imagine. You are in a white room, simple, doorless. You don't know where the room ends, but you have been sucked inside. You can hear nothing beyond it. Your body is light and you can't set your feet down. You drift, you fall, empty, massless. You open your mouth, but you can't scream. Yet, while there, you are still considered to exist. It is difficult, child. Difficult. That is why I prepare a bottle for each mother.'

'A bottle?'

She offers her thin hands, inviting Gita to follow. Something has drawn them closer; Gita no longer fears her. The two are like bats, relying on each other because the rays of the sun have penetrated their cave. They have to understand each other.

Sumarni leads her to a room inside the house. A normal room, containing a bed with dull beige sheets. Beside it stands a timber wardrobe. The wardrobe isn't especially wide, but it reaches to the ceiling. How odd. All it contains is empty sauce bottles, perhaps hundreds. Gita asks why she keeps so many.

The old woman shakes her head. 'These bottles are not empty. Each one holds a scream.'

'A scream?'

'Yes.'

'Why do the screams need to be kept safe?'

'A mother's scream dies with her baby. They are no longer able to speak. No one will want to hear. They are troublemakers, pariahs. What I do, child, is offer a home for the screams. If I didn't, the scream would evaporate and leave the woman mute for ever.' Sumarni takes a bottle from the bottom shelf and cradles it. 'This one belonged to a woman from my village. She came to me fifteen years ago, when she was very young. She's dead now, so the bottle can be opened. Do you want to hear it?'

Before Gita can decide, Sumarni is already turning the cap of the golden bottle. In the distance, Gita hears a wrenching howl. The death cry of a hound. The wail comes ever closer. No. The cry is her own. She is on top of a cliff, her hands and feet bound, her flesh scraping against a sharp rock face. Suddenly, she sees a figure above her, soaring. The creature has a skull with long pointed ears, and its black robes obstruct the sky. Gita sees only darkness. The creature descends slowly towards her until their bodies touch. It is so thin, but its weight makes her gasp. She struggles. The face of the one in the black robes inches closer, until its hard, cold lips graze Gita's. Its mouth opens. It emits a rancid stench and a deafening screech. Gita turns away, clamping her eyes shut.

Sumarni hastily reseals the bottle. She puts her arm around Gita's shoulder and strokes her hair. She leads her guest slowly out of the room.

Gita sits on the pale green sofa in the living room, biting her lips, covering her eyes with her hands.

Sumarni sits next to her.

'Did you see it? I keep every noise, so that it doesn't place the kiss of death on them, so that they don't disappear unburied.'

'I really have to go now, really... have to —' Gita stammers. 'Thank you for everything.'

Gita says goodbye to Sumarni, and goes to the door. Outside, the rain begins to pelt down.

'Your house is so sombre. Now I know why no light enters. But understanding doesn't make everything simple.'

'Child, you forgot something.' Sumarni is leaning against the door and clutching a bottle. 'This is yours.'

Gita shakes her head. 'You're mistaken.' She shakes her head more firmly and quickens her pace. She doesn't want to look back.

Sumarni smiles sadly.

'I'll be sure to hold on to it,' she says. She is quite certain her guest hears her. 'My door is always open for you.'

**Maybe you don't believe in the supernatural. I didn't either,** until my best friend Herjuno's life was upended by a mocking, mystical force.

One night, Herjuno had a strange dream. He saw a man dressed in sumptuous, glittering robes. The man sat, cross-legged and eyes closed, on a tapestry embroidered with gold threads. A sharp aroma wafted from the offerings that flanked the bed. Torches provided the only light. A dome, like a cloche, stood above the scene, supported by teak pillars. Soon came thunderbolts, rain, a fierce storm. With a roar, the gusts burst the door open and a greenish glow flooded the room.

A searing light then forced Herjuno to avert his eyes. When he turned back, he saw a woman seated on a litter that was being shouldered by an entourage of bare-chested young men. The litter featured a carved dragon's head, topped by a diamond-studded crown. The woman was the most exquisite Herjuno had ever seen. He could smell the strands of jasmine that tied the ringlets of her shimmering hair. But it wasn't hair. The shimmering came from the eyes of snakes, black, cold, slippery. She was wrapped in an emerald robe replete with crimson roses. Flower petals lay scattered about like lips in full bloom.

The woman clapped her hands twice. The young men lowered the litter, bowed their heads and then turned into fireflies. They flitted about before darting away and vanishing. Herjuno saw the man's eyes open. The woman approached him and straddled his lap. His chin was raised and his eyes stared straight ahead. The woman stripped off her emerald robe, which slid to the floor. Herjuno held his breath.

Their lovemaking was magnificent. They coupled three times. A fourth. Herjuno didn't want to budge. The woman knelt in front of the man. Herjuno felt himself soar high into the sky. From above, he observed the rain become a fountain. It soaked into the carpet of verdant rice fields, making them fertile.

Midnight. Herjuno woke. He glanced at his wife lying beside him in her frumpy nightgown. She was lying on her stomach, fast asleep. An anticlimax if ever there was one. The mattress beneath Herjuno was damp.

The following day, Herjuno called me. Could I meet him for lunch, so he could tell me his dream? Clearly he wanted to know its meaning. Herjuno was old-fashioned. He had grown up in a big city but belief in the occult ran in his family. I smiled away his anxiety. 'It was just a sex dream, man. Not getting to unclog the pipes enough lately, huh?'

Herjuno punched my arm.

'Or else you get off from watching other people do it. Or you're longing for some wild sex. Threesomes. Orgies.'

He punched me again but this time laughed, too.

Privately, I thought the dream reflected the two years Herjuno had spent stuck in a dull marriage. The fountain that fertilised the fields represented a demand to spread his seed.

Herjuno's marriage was a surprise, even to me, and we've been best friends since secondary school. 'Shit happens, man.' He shrugged when he told me.

'My God, Jun...' I tapped my forehead. 'Don't tell me this is what that test of yours has led to.'

Before being imprisoned in his marital jail, Herjuno was an adventurer in love. He was traditional: he championed the values of feudal patriarchy, updated. He considered the attributes of a modern knight to be the latest car (instead of a handsome steed), money from his old man to fund a start-up (instead of inherited land) and slim girls in shapewear (instead of virgins in corsets). Herjuno boasted of all these.

All his life, Herjuno had known two types of women and he dated them simultaneously: those who were virgins and those who were not. For him, non-virgins existed to play around with. Meanwhile, his true vocation was testing virgins. If, during their courtship, a girl 'surrendered her chastity to him' (this was a favourite phrase of Herjuno's – pretty anachronistic for the twenty-first century, huh?), that meant she didn't resist temptation, which meant she failed his test, which meant she was unworthy of becoming his wife.

Always leave room for the best: that was another of my friend's catchphrases. I noticed that whenever he ate he saved his favourite side dish for last, only touching it once he had finished his rice and other dishes.

Dewi was a female of the virgin category who, predictably, failed his test. But she also fell pregnant. Yet, I think what happened was no catastrophe. Herjuno, the larger-than-life knight who had never even heard of, let alone contemplated, pulling himself up by his own bootstraps, accepted a rotting durian because Dewi's father owned a major corporation with mining interests.

Two weeks later, I received an invitation that proudly announced their names: Herjuno Bambang Prasojo, MBA and Dewi Wulandari, BEcon. The marriage reception was held in the ballroom of a hotel that Dewi's father had invested in. The usual reception halls were booked until the end of the following year. Among the wedding guests were General So-and-so, Minister Such-and-such and other faces that regularly greet the public on TV screens.

Their child was born seven months after the festive marriage. From that point on, Dewi Wulandari, BEcon, became a consummate housewife. She cared for the baby, breastfeeding until the child was two. Herjuno entrusted his own small enterprise to his younger brother, a recent university graduate, while he accepted an offer as a director in his father-in-law's corporation – proof that his MBA stood for more than Married By Accident.

My friend was now desperately assuring me that something was going to happen. The dream was too real, too vivid, and Herjuno believed that a dream that leaves a question mark after waking is a sign.

'Besides, Gus,' he added, 'I've got a genuine problem.'

Maybe the dream was a warning, but it could also have been a solution.

Herjuno's belief in the occult grew. Now it was buttressed by not only his own superstitious family but his wife's. Opening a new business? A palaver with a psychic was a prerequisite. Confirming a major deal? A horoscope analysis was de rigueur. So it was no wonder that in response to his bizarre dream, Herjuno resolved to contact Ki Joko Kuncoro, trusted medium to his extended family.

—

Once upon a time, there lived a wondrously beautiful princess. She begged her enchantress grandmother to make her beauty eternal. Ageless. Immortal. Her grandmother granted her request on the condition that the girl agree to become a lelembut, a troublemaking spirit. Then, for that glow of unfading beauty, the girl plunged into the sea and surrendered to the lapping of the seductive waves. She was now alone and friendless, but she possessed a palace in plain view of all and an assemblage of ghostly warriors. She was Kanjeng Ratu Kidul, Queen of the South Sea.

One day, the Queen spied the founding sultan of Mataram, Panembahan Senopati, meditating, pleading for the prosperity of his people. So powerful was her desire that the sea raged, boiling, and the fish were hurled up onto dry land. This caused the Queen to reveal her form. It is unclear whether she was led to do so by a mortal threat to the creatures of the deep or by Senopati's charm and power but, in the end, they came to know each other. Kanjeng Ratu was prepared to help Panembahan Senopati achieve prosperity on the condition that Panembahan and his heirs would serve as her consorts. An agreement was reached and peace descended upon the mortal realm once more.

Since that time, the members of the lineage of Senopati are destined to serve as consorts to the Queen of the South Sea. The princes of the Surakarta Kraton have always held a special bond with this lelembut. Even the site of the union of body and soul with the Queen was deemed a special place, the Sangga Buwana Tower.

The marriage of the Queen and Senopati meant a harmony of water and land, heaven and earth, linggam and yoni. The balance imparted fertility to the Sultanate of Mataram and yoked the South Sea to it.

—

Psychic Ki Joko Kuncoro's workspace was covered with Javanese daggers, old books, and photographs taken with the rich and famous. I knew because Herjuno had asked me to come along with him. The psychic's client list was nothing to be sneezed at: it included prominent businessmen and government officials. The psychic was dressed in black and looked as if he kept up with the times. On his desk stood a computer with internet access. Maybe googling information was quicker than seeking divine inspiration.

According to Ki Joko Kuncoro, Herjuno's vision was no mere dream. Nor was the beautiful woman an ordinary woman, but the Queen of the South Sea. Meeting her would lead to one of two outcomes: happiness or havoc.

'She is zealous, merciless,' he said. 'Everyone knows that each year the South Sea demands life. Countless victims have been dragged beneath the waves. Not only those who dare to swim, but also those who simply sit and play with grains of sand. Before their death, they might hear a song, honey-sweet and seductive. A siren's call. Then, as if sleepwalking, they heed the call of the sea. Some bodies are never found.'

'I've heard of her. The princess who so desired everlasting beauty that she traded her life for the fate of shadows,' said Herjuno. It sounded dreadful to me.

'Actually, there's another tale,' said Ki Joko. 'The Sundanese version. In the era of the Pajajaran kingdom, a princess suffered from a hideous affliction of the skin, an unnatural disease that could bring misfortune to the entire land. She was expelled from the kingdom by her ashamed family. She committed suicide, drowning herself in the clear waters of the sea. Water can salve scabies and sin. One day, when a royal entourage was praying in Pelabuhan Ratu, a beautiful princess appeared. The Hideous One had been transformed into a queen of the spirits and now held her throne in the South Sea.'

Herjuno nodded, frowning. I was startled. This story was no cheerier. Women so lacking in confidence that they kill themselves are no less worrisome than those obsessed with beauty.

'So, she fell in love with Senopati, as he prayed for the prosperity of his people?' I asked.

'Yes, but maybe more than that. Senopati was meditating, gathering all his mental energy, seeking a strategy to oppose the northern kingdom. No one truly knows what happened. It is said that for three days and three nights, the Queen shared secrets with Senopati: political secrets, military secrets and carnal secrets.'

Three days and three nights. She certainly knew how to set the chess pieces of statecraft in motion.

'And you must remember,' Ki Joko warned, 'never doubt her strength. She is a jealous woman; it is taboo for maidens of Kidul to wear orange or chequered cloth in the sea. It makes her angry, and when she is angry, she will devour anything. Livestock. Children. Babies. She is like Calon Arang, master of black magic. Her rage is blind. She can destroy you.'

'What should I do, then?' Herjuno asked.

Ki Joko shook his head. 'History will repeat itself. Don't you see? Senopati gained power by merging with Kanjeng Ratu Kidul, body and soul.'

The Queen of the South Sea's marriage to Senopati meant the fortification of Mataram's territory as far as the boundless South

Sea. A legitimation of his power. Who would not be terrified to hear of the Queen's uncanny forces standing behind the Sultanate of Mataram? The lesson behind all this: don't make enemies of wild horses. Ride them.

Ki Joko muttered something. After a while, I realised that he was reciting Javanese poetry:

> *Nenggih Kangjeng Ratu Kidul*
> *Ndedel nggayuh nggegana*
> *Umara marak maripih*
> *Sor prabawa lan wong angung Ngeksiganda*

Herjuno and I looked at each other.

'Do I need to go to the South Sea and make offerings?' Herjuno whispered to me.

Ki Joko noticed our hesitation. I turned to Herjuno.

'Do you understand the verse, Jun? *The Queen of the South Sea / Flying high in the air / Came to worship / Lost authority to the Sultan of Mataram.*'

'Herjuno, listen,' Ki Joko interrupted. 'Before the marriage of the Queen and the next Mataram king, nine women will dance and summon him. The Queen will appear in miraculous fashion in the form of the tenth dancer. The most beautiful dancer of all. She can transform into anything. An animal, the wind, a woman. Before you can catch her, she has already changed shape. She can assume an incarnated form.'

'Do you mean to say that there's an incarnation of the Queen of the South Sea now, in our era?'

He nodded. 'If you're able to grab hold of her saddle, she will take you places you've never imagined.'

If you're able.

Herjuno felt he had understood. Like Senopati, who perpetu-ated the power of Mataram by marrying the Queen of the South Sea, Herjuno had to serve as the Queen's consort.

'If you meet her, recite these words: *Gaze up to Heavenly Father, bow down to Mother Earth.* And remember: never, ever under-estimate her.'

———

After his visit to Ki Joko, Herjuno took notice of all the women he met, hoping to identify the Queen of the South Sea. She would need to be a strong, charismatic woman. The search revived his energy. He lit up whenever he spoke about the array of beautiful women he suspected might be the Queen. I didn't pay much at-tention until one day we were at a reception commemorating the rollout of a new car model. The company throwing the reception belonged to one of Herjuno's acquaintances.

We met a woman who wore sleek black trousers and a tight black leather jacket. Her frame was slim but powerful. She re-sembled a scorpion. Luxurious, shimmering, intimidating. Dark grey make-up swept up around her gorgeous eyes, making them stand out. When she spoke, her voice was as velvety as a Bloody Mary.

She greeted us confidently and beckoned us over to chat. She was a lawyer. That was as much detail as I heard because Herjuno quickly signalled me to leave the two of them alone. He obviously thought she was the modern-day incarnation of the Queen that Ki Joko had told him about. I excused myself and slipped off behind a table of canapes. A waiter passed in front of me with a tray of drinks. I chose a Cabernet Sauvignon and held the glass to my nose. Notes of raspberry mixed with sandalwood.

Almost an hour later, Herjuno came over.

'That woman isn't just any lawyer,' he whispered. 'She's got her eye on what my company is up to.'

'You mean your father-in-law's company?'

'She knows about what's going on with the waste.'

A few months ago, a researcher had disclosed his findings to Herjuno. The marine zone near the waste disposal site of his father-in-law's company was contaminated with hazardous compounds. Arsenic and cyanide polluted the water. Fish were growing tumours, dying. Residents nearby complained of itchy rashes all over their bodies. Pregnant women miscarried. The researcher was insisting on publishing his report in a prominent newspaper. After a lengthy set of back-and-forth discussions, he agreed not to go public with his findings in exchange for a considerable payoff. At least the money would guarantee his research projects for five years.

'How did she find out?'

'Rumours are circulating among environmentalists. Maybe the researcher didn't keep his word. But there might be others out there looking into the issue too.'

'How many billions do you have to give away to keep them all quiet?'

Herjuno shook his head. 'That's not the way it's done.'

I found out later that a journalist was going to publish an article about the contaminated waters that week and that the news had reached the lawyer's ears from the editor of a bi-weekly magazine. According to Herjuno, though, the woman he had just met promised to help him wage a media war.

She would use her influence to have several researchers and journalists create competing accounts. If possible, they would hold workshops at universities. The validity of the research could always be thrown into doubt and there were always powerful people available to distract the public.

I listened to Herjuno carefully. He had mentioned the waste issue before but I had no idea that it had become this complicated. Still, why was this woman concerned?

'It's not just my people who have interests here, Gus,' my friend said. 'Other parties will get hurt if this case blows up. And she's representing those parties.'

I asked how much money she wanted. Herjuno looked at me with a knowing grin.

'Jun?'

'We haven't reached an explicit agreement about compensation yet. But I promised to take her home tonight.'

It couldn't be that simple. I worried that Herjuno was being naïve. And, after all, if she really was the Queen of the South Sea, wouldn't she be pissed off about the contamination?

'Relax, Gus.' He put his arm around me. 'What was it that the Queen of the South Sea wanted after she gave away that bountiful power of hers?'

'A wedding proposal?'

I was joking, but my friend's leering grin suggested more. He was convinced that the problem would be solved by an influential woman. He had found his queen. A queen who always appeared when fish were in their death throes.

———

Herjuno needed my help.

That's what he told me when we met up the following day. We chose a café decorated in a retro style.

'So what happened last night?'

Herjuno laughed gleefully, 'Hey, don't go jumping to conclusions!'

Even after so many years of a friendship, he still bullshitted me.

'Nothing too much,' he went on. 'Not yet.' My friend paused. Then he looked at me seriously. 'She invited me to a hotel later tonight. She's going to give me the names of a bunch of influential media people who can help my position.'

'And you won't be talking in a restaurant, will you?'

Herjuno laughed so long and hard that his ears flushed. I didn't need to hear his explanation. I imagined the scorpion woman twisting and turning. She could probably lure any man she wanted into bed. It sounded like she was already mingling public duties and private pleasures. How befitting of the Queen of the South Sea.

'I told my wife there was a meeting at Puncak.'

'Jun, she would see right through that. It's her father's company.'

'She doesn't have a clue about work stuff.' Herjuno said. 'If she asks you, just tell her that there's a crucial meeting on. With important clients. They only invited me. All good?'

I sipped my coffee. It wouldn't be the first time I had lied on Herjuno's behalf.

'Anyway, this is a rescue mission. If I don't do it, my in-laws' company, and their reputation, will be at stake.' Herjuno made excuses.

Herjuno's wife was really straitlaced, even if not exactly boring. She wouldn't be suspicious. All she thought about was their kid. She'd never been interested in taking part in social functions with other CEO wives clutching their thousand-dollar handbags. She only left home to take their daughter to preschool or shop at the supermarket. Once a month, she would go to see the symphony orchestra, the ballet or the theatre. She didn't like cafés or clubs. Even her phone rarely rang; she had few friends.

'It's Friday night by the Javanese calendar,' Herjuno said.

'So?'

'I'm going to make love to her,' he said. 'And say the mantra.'

*Bow down to the Heavenly Father.*

I was afraid all of a sudden.

'The woman might have other plans, Herjuno.'

If there was any truth to the legend, Herjuno was dealing with no ordinary woman.

'That's why I asked for your help.'

So Herjuno had dragged me into a dangerous stream. I might drown along with him.

———

That night, we left for the hotel separately. I set out first and waited for them in the hotel lobby, holding a newspaper up before my face like a film character and feeling ridiculous. Herjuno appeared two hours later with his gorgeous lawyer friend. He had paid for room number 324 for me, not far from his room, 320. I peeked at them from behind the newspaper. We pretended not to see each other. Herjuno had an arm wrapped around her waist. She was wearing a short, tight dress, black and dazzling. I looked at Herjuno and thought of a child impatient to play with a scorpion: he knows it's poisonous, yet that only adds to the excitement. I was there to stand guard.

I went up to my room and worked on my laptop. Time inched towards midnight.

Fed up with working, I switched on the television. A thriller about a group of teenagers chased by a psychopath was on. After a narrow series of escapes, one kid took a bath, relaxing after all the tension. The mistake the victim always makes is breathing a sigh of relief. The boy didn't realise the killer was nearby and drawing closer, axe in hand. He was wearing a mask. His black gloves drew the curtain away and brought the axe down. The wretched kid screamed. An ear-splitting scream. The axe fell again and again.

I winced, imagining an axe chopping through my flesh.

The bathtub became a sea of red. The killer had won the day.

The teenager in the movie fell face-first into the water, dead. But the scream lingered, piercing the walls. My heart raced.

The scream was real. It was Herjuno.

I was caught off guard. I'm no hero but I was frightened for my best friend; that woman, the scorpion, had stung him.

I ran to his room. None of the other guests did the same. Maybe they thought the sounds were only the cries of a couple making love.

I knocked at the door, calling Herjuno. I still hoped he was joking. But the cries got louder. The door was locked from the inside. My hands were sweaty. I pounded on the door. Should I break it down?

Before I could decide, it clicked open. I barged in to find my friend kneeling on the floor, clutching one hand with the other. There were crimson splotches on his unbuttoned white shirt. Something awful had happened and he had used what was left of his strength to open the door.

'Jun!'

His left hand was covering his right. Blood was flowing, soaking into the carpet.

Herjuno fainted. When his hand fell away, I saw that his middle finger was missing.

I raised my head and saw the face of the woman who had maimed him.

A woman wreathed with flowers. Her luxurious dress billowed in waves. The Queen. A gust of wind flung the balcony door open and leaves swirled into the room.

My eyes smarted from the dust. I could just make out the sound of breaking surf. What struck me most wasn't her glittering appearance but her familiar face. Not the face of a dramatic, influential woman, but the face of an ordinary woman I'd gazed at across the dinner table.

Dewi, Herjuno's wife.

She fixed me with her stare. I realised, then, that she was holding a chain. A frightening creature was bound to it. A giant scorpion.

I backed towards the door, in terror, but unable to look away. Then, the Queen turned, and she and the scorpion flew through the window and disappeared.

—

That fateful night stole not only Herjuno's middle finger but also his sanity. He is now under intensive supervision by a psychiatrist. He babbles on about the Queen of the South Sea. They think he had a breakdown because his wife ran off with his daughter, leaving him only a letter. Dewi's signature was stamped on it. In the letter, she wrote of how devastated she was to learn that her husband was having an affair and asked that he not try to find her. Very sentimental. The paper contained no trace of the Queen of the South Sea, no indication of her disguise as Dewi all this time.

It is getting to the point where Herjuno might be locked up in an asylum. Nobody believes his story.

Only I know the truth.

But I say nothing. I'm not sure why. Sometimes I think it's because I don't want to be labelled crazy too. Sometimes I think it's because I sympathise with Dewi or the Queen. I'm not certain whose side I'm on any more.

I've had time to wonder why Herjuno's life has been spared. Why only his middle finger was sacrificed and not his soul. If someone goes missing on the beach at Parangtritis, people believe that the Queen has taken a victim. To become one of her ghostly warriors, perhaps. I've come to the conclusion that Herjuno didn't mean enough to the Queen of the South Sea to receive that blessing of eternal life.

Sometimes, voices from ancient times echo in my ears.

*Gung pra peri perayangan ejim sarawi*
*Sang Sinom Prabu Rara yekti gedhe dhewe.*

*Read Saras backwards and you will find me.*

*We come from the same place, cramped, dark, wet, red. But she doesn't want me because she thinks I suckle at the breast of a she-wolf.*

———

I never imagined I would become a secretary. When I was little, when people asked me what I wanted to be I said, 'a doctor' just like thousands of other kids. But my mum noticed how diligent and orderly I was. I loved making catalogues of my school subjects, a budget for how I would spend my allowance, grocery lists. I was crazy about categorising. In my room I separated my music cassettes into different boxes according to genre. I could even tell you what clothes I would wear two weeks from Friday. Mum mocked me, 'You're better suited to being a secretary than a doctor.'

After high school I went to a secretarial academy. I did it in part to maximise my potential and in part because to be a doctor you have to like biology and the only thing I liked about biology was taxonomy. In the end, I realised that my decision to study at Tarakanita Secretarial Academy was the right one; I graduated with top marks.

———

*I live in the caves of darkest night, enveloped in grey mist. I know neither morning nor dew. I dare not challenge the light; I'm not like anyone else. I am obsessed with red. Red pooling in continuous flow, reminiscent of fresh fish.*

*I thirst for blood.*

*I am a black butterfly with wings of velvet. I dart into corridors, drawn by the vortex of the night. She doesn't know my pain, my moans, my passion. She closes all the windows to drive away my ungainly thirst.*

I started work in a consulting company. I always ironed my work jacket and skirt as smooth as could be. They matched the office's cool mahogany floors and walls, which were a shade of chocolate milk. Brown is a classic colour; it always looks elegant. Want to look more professional? Wear brown or black. Funny, I used to think dark colours stood for evil and bright colours for good.

*Sometimes I seek rats, dogs, anything at all. I am too weak to open my eyes. I can't bear it, I'm so thirsty. If only I could exchange my soul for blood.*

I was secretary to the marketing manager. My desk, always neat and tidy, was just outside my boss's door. His name was Irwan. He was young, handsome, rich, intelligent. Of course, he had one flaw: a wife. This was a problem for him because he

98

had to work desperately to cover up his many affairs. (At least, that's what I heard on my first day.) It was a problem for me too because I had to keep my distance; the intense familiarity of our daily interactions might give him the wrong impression. I'd heard of office romances but I'd never had the desire to take part in one.

Irwan came from a wealthy family, which was probably why he abused his power in small ways. He asked me to draft proposal letters for a side project of his that had nothing to do with work. Once I had to leave the office just to pay his credit card bills. I knew I had the right to protest, but, for the time being, I kept quiet.

———

'Do you have plans after work?'

I lifted my head. Irwan was wearing a red tie, which peeked from his conservative suit jacket. There was something terribly wrong about that tie. Maybe its colour was too bright. It didn't match the atmosphere at all. The office was full of dull colours.

*Red is sultry. Red coagulates and sticks like chewing gum. Red demands realisation, real-I-sation, it cannot be put off, cannot be flushed down into a sewer.*

'Saras?'

'No, no plans.'

'Then come and have a coffee with me.'

When you work for someone, you get used to imperative sentences.

I was trying to guess at the meaning behind that coffee. What he meant was coffee in a cup and saucer in an air-conditioned space, not coffee served up black in a glass at a roadside stall with grounds floating in it. What he meant was to share in a ritual that belonged to a specific class and had a specific purpose – to establish a relationship, or maybe to do some networking. Very attractive for career development, but I wasn't interested in getting closer to a married man.

*Hypocrite.*

I wondered if there might be consequences if I refused.

*She wants him, but doesn't want to be the one to shoulder the blame.*

'I've been tasked with an extra assignment,' he said. 'The managing director needs a special report finished by tomorrow. I hope you can help.'

Irwan seemed to notice my hesitation. He stressed that the invitation was a professional one. After thinking it over, I accepted.

*I am the sibling who shares warmth with you in that narrow, red space. I know how in high school you read a cheap porn novel about a secretary who went into her boss's office not wearing any underwear. You are crass, crazed, crimson. Come on, crack! Don't you dream of satisfying the animal wildness under that sophisticated skirt of yours?*

So we went to a cafe that played fifties jazz. Tucked away in the dim light, we sat on a red velvet sofa so big I sunk into it. Without the coffee, I might have become drowsy. Why did Irwan choose a place like this to discuss an office project?

*A brothel –*

*A butterfly like me prefers the dim, the dusky, the delusion, the dream. A festive house in a forest filled with wolves. You will never understand until you step inside.*

We talked for two hours. Espresso gave way to cappuccino. For half an hour, he discussed the special report. Ella Fitzgerald and her golden voice were a seductive distraction but I listened attentively and took notes, being the highly trained professional that I am. Then he asked, 'Do you still live with your parents?'

I was stunned by the question. I told him I lived alone. Said that my parents lived outside the city and that I was an only child. He told me that he was, too.

Then began the dangerous ritual of clichés about an unhappy marriage. That his wife was busy pursuing her own ambitions, that they had no child to bind them.

I had to put an end to this. He was looking for prey.

*I am too. Is anyone willing to surrender a soul?*

'I have to go,' I said.

It wasn't all that late, yet Irwan wanted to escort me home. I said it wasn't necessary but he insisted.

'Okay, as far as the front gate.'

*The man knows you live alone.*

*You and I are lonely creatures. I absorb life that is in the throes of death because red is almost finished, fatal, a full stop.*

He asked to use the bathroom, so I let him in.

*Enter. Scale the fence, O prowlers. Let us leap, do not skulk. Look what you can taste in the orchard. I followed because I too am a thief, a pilferer of life and death, and I will make you a ghost.*

He sat in my wicker chair, drinking a glass of water. He opened a button of his shirt and loosened his tie — a tie that was totally wrong.

*Look at the man's neck. Do you like vanilla ice-cream? Taste its iciness with your tongue and it will melt in your mouth.*

He spoke my name. It was a murmur, but I caught what he said afterwards: 'We always knew what would happen between us.'

I was shaking. My fears had come true. But I was professional; I knew to reject him, to throw him out if necessary.

Yet I felt him getting closer and closer. Cologne and cigarette smoke wafted from his neatly trimmed hair. I felt as if —

*Sucked in?*

*Atop the ice-cream sits a shiny, round cherry. The fruit tempts, challenges danger. Will I fall? But I want it so much. I imbibe life.*

*His neck is so beautiful. And I am so thirsty for blood.*

———

8:00 am. The phone rings.

'Hello, Saras?' A woman's voice on the other end. 'Irwan's not answering his phone. He has a meeting with a client at eleven — could you remind him as soon as you see him?'

**I never knew her real name.**

She was imperious from our first meeting, when she told me, 'This is difficult work.' She spoke from a shiny black chair, her back to me. I had the feeling the chair was hiding a truly powerful figure who wanted to keep her identity secret. A mafia boss, I decided, one who wouldn't let me see anything but the smoke trails rising from her cigarette.

In her office was a glass cabinet. It contained opaque clues about her. Chemistry books, children's stories, some VHS videotapes. I suspected she wasn't a businesswoman and was puzzled as to why she couldn't just hire almost anyone at random for the job; nothing in the key selection criteria stood out. Male. Minimum height 175 cm. Of sound mind. Not fat. What specifications there were emphasised appearance. Public relations, maybe? But why was she willing to pay so much? My situation meant I had little time for suspicions.

I was there because I was desperate. Predictions of a prolonged impact after the recent financial crisis had been rife, but I'd never imagined I would fall victim. At the beginning of the year, the promise of a pay hike drew me to a smaller company, owned by the son of el número uno in this country. Two months ago, though, murmurs about downsizing had started, and then I was sent packing.

After that came a series of unexpected setbacks. No company would take me on. My wife sold off her handbags one by one, which of course fuelled gossip about my hard luck. The crisis soon became an ugly test to discover who was in the outermost circle and would get bounced, and who — thanks to a wise selection of friends — remained on the inside. Like magic, most of those I'd assumed would spread a safety net for me disappeared. I became a leper.

My beautiful wife didn't complain, but I knew she missed joining friends for dinners at restaurants or renting villas at weekends. When I heard that the ex-wife of a wealthy business-man was looking for someone to help out on a project, I sent a letter of application and my resume. The role itself was fuzzy, but it offered double my previous salary.

'Six men have tried this work and they all failed,' the woman warned from behind the black chair.

She was yet to arrive at the point so I broached it politely. 'What kind of business do you run, madam?'

She sighed, softly at first, yet soon the sigh turned into laugh-ter. Not the laughter of a colleague making you feel comfortable but the degrading laughter of a tyrant.

'Oh, this work is important. Your services are sorely needed.'

For a while she said nothing more. Then, in language stripped of formality, she stated what she wanted. It made my face flush. I felt silly. She remained motionless and stopped exhaling her smoke.

The woman wanted to pay me to have sex with her.

My confidence collapsed. Not because I'd never been involved in a transaction like this – the whims of youth had taken me to several call girls. Yet there is a big difference between paying and being paid. And this strange woman, who wouldn't even look me in the face, wanted to make me her whore.

I felt like I was being trampled underfoot. If only I'd high-tailed it out of there. But the threat of a future as a pariah made me anxious. I was an economic castaway and my losses could only keep coming – friends, car, house. Maybe even my beautiful wife.

I took a deep breath. 'I'll try my best.'

She hadn't finished. 'You haven't asked for details. I love stories. I love acting them out even more.'

I came to wish I'd taken that statement as another warning.

Unable to guess what she was insinuating, I asked if she had any particular story in mind. 'The Beauty of Ancol Bridge,' she said, naming a well-known ghost tale. Reading the confusion in my face, she explained herself calmly. 'I want you to rape me.'

I felt myself go limp. She repeated her request; I wasn't up to hearing it twice. I had swallowed my pride in agreeing to whore myself out. Now she wanted to call me a rapist.

'Come on,' she said. 'It will only be make believe.'

She outlined the scenario. She would give me the uniform of a Civil Defence guard and have me hide in a wardrobe in her room. Dressed as the Beauty of Ancol Bridge, she would come into the room after prayers, still veiled. As she was removing her veil, I was supposed to leap from the wardrobe, grab her, and begin by tearing off her blouse.

I figured that the woman was out of her mind. But I was desperate. I asked her to increase the pay a tad reluctantly, out of pride. But when I considered that someone like her had no shame, I quickly overcame my hesitance.

She agreed, laughing. She even told me she would pay half my salary up front. She seemed pleased to have filled the position with such a promising candidate.

Without turning around, she waved a contract at me. I swallowed. On it was printed the stipulation that I was responsible for completing my work 'professionally and efficiently', while following a 'flexible' schedule for three months. Listed beneath were my name and hers. Her name seemed familiar but I couldn't immediately pin it down. I picked up the pen, my palms sweating.

As soon as I scrawled my signature, she twisted the black chair around and looked straight at me.

The woman's face was like a rough chunk of meat. It was difficult to say where her nose ended and her cheeks began. Her left eye was swollen and red, like an inflamed ulcer. If it wasn't for her straight hair I wouldn't have been sure she was human. She was a tumour come to life, covered in pustules and obscene.

I prayed that God would rescue me from this horrible joke but it was too late. I had already shoved the thick wad of rupiah into my bag and now fled the office, jumped into my car and drove away, feeling frantic. A car behind me honked and pulled past, its occupant cursing. That's when I realised what had escaped me earlier. The name on the contract, Siti Ariah, was the name of the Beauty of Ancol Bridge. I'd signed a contract with a devil woman.

——

That damned contract landed me in the darkness of a sturdy teak wardrobe with carvings on both doors. I was sweating beneath the guard uniform she'd instructed me to wear. I held my breath when I heard footsteps enter the room. My heart had never pounded as hard as it did on that first day of work. I didn't feel like a rapist – I was more like a submissive bull, fearful of being led into the slaughterhouse.

She and I were close, separated by nothing but the timber of the antique wardrobe. It was time. *One, two, three.* I burst through the door. She was dressed in batik and a white Javanese blouse embroidered with small flowers. She was removing her veil. My throat constricted when I caught sight of her wasted face.

She instructed me to say her name. *Ariah.* Her eyes narrowed. She faced me, impatient, as I stood fixed in place before her. I knew I had to act fast. My hands trembled as I took her shoulders and started shaking them. She slapped me hard.

'Say you want to rape me, you son of a bitch.'

The slap jolted me, drove me to throw her onto the bed. Ariah writhed and kicked at my thighs. Breathing hard, I pinned her hands and ripped off her blouse.

When I laid eyes on her body I gasped. It wasn't mutilated at all. I'd never beheld such curves. What kind of joke was this? The scene was bizarre, disorienting, like an unfinished painting. I felt ill.

If nothing else, the sight of her body made my own react: I became the son of a bitch she wanted. Unwilling to let her prey escape, she ordered me to look her in the eyes. I ravaged her, not once turning away from that horrid face of hers, sobbing all the while.

She took no pity on me and urged me to rougher heights. She spewed curses that reddened my ears. Every time she opened her mouth, every time she gasped and moaned, I felt like I was being stabbed. Over and over again. Those eyes – those asymmetrical eyes that refused to close – were the worst. They widened, making me feel like I was fucking a putrid fish cast up on dry land. Cold, scaly, twitching.

Everything happened fast. My brain went into overdrive. I thought: just finish it off and you're free. At the end of our little role play, my face was close to hers. She smiled, cruel and content, as I caught the odour of an animal that has just died. An unbearable, bitter taste spread in my mouth. Without a chance to flee, I vomited my guts up onto the floor.

Ariah got to her feet and slipped on her robe. I was still gasping for breath when she stood over me and folded her arms. She looked as if she were faking sympathy towards a slave. She laughed hysterically, then said, 'Not too shabby. Now go and clean up your puke. And come back tomorrow.'

———

And so it went. I kept visiting Ariah's house, lurking in her wardrobe, then attacking and 'raping' her. For the whole first week, I had no appetite. The inflamed tumour of her face loomed on my dinner plate in lumps, mocking me. I threw up again and again. And wept. One night, as my wife applied the face cream that nourished her beauty, she asked what was so draining about my new job.

'I just need to get used to it,' I lied.

At night, I tried to make love to my beautiful wife to forget what I had been through during the day. But there was always a point when her perfect features dissolved into the revolting face of Ariah. The fragrance of my wife's body – a soft, clean lavender – evaporated, only to be replaced by the stench of animals at market, of stagnant water churning with blood.

After the first time, I thought I would quit by the end of the week. Instead, I was surprised to find within myself an astonishing tenacity. By the second week, I'd learned self-deception: yes, her face was a horror, but my misery would come to an end once I collected all my money and found another job. I inured myself to disgust, habituated myself to rape, as though I'd always longed for such ugliness.

In the third week, I started to note major changes within myself. I started to believe in the mantra that she commanded me to memorise: *Ariah, Ariah, I want to pulverise you.* Not only could I perform my role as the rapist of a hideous woman without nausea, but now I could stare into her eyes, searching them for an explosive depravity.

To be sure, this change instilled terror in me. Not only of her but of myself. I didn't dare confirm it, but over time my performance ceased to be a question of adaptation. Something else was involved – an uncanny impulse beyond my control.

Secretly, I began to enjoy my work.

I know it's hard to fathom. God knows I was worried about my sanity. But the woman made love as if possessed and this wore off on me. I decided Ariah had violated our contract: often, I felt like I was the one being raped.

But I allowed it. Even longed for it.

How wretched was that human tumour. Every recess of my brain pulsed with pleasure whenever she clawed and hit and slapped me. A thrilling jolt surged through me when she roughed me up. I held her down because I knew she would kick me. The more I internalised my role as the rapist, the more viciously she treated me. I slapped her because I wanted her to box my ears, harder, over and over. I said I wanted to rape her to encourage that savage voice of hers to lacerate me with dirty, guttural whispers.

My pact with the devil dragged me into a universe I'd never known. She awoke in me desires I didn't recognise. A desire to be degraded. The woman infected me with her disease. Questions that I dared not ask gnawed at me. How did she become such a terrifying creature? Why, how, could she repulse me so and yet draw me in at the same time?

——

I don't know if it was because she was satisfied with my work or because she realised we shared an illness, but Ariah started to treat me like a human being. I say that because up until then she had behaved as if I was a dog. She made me satisfy her five times a day. The next morning, while I was still slumbering next to my wife, she would order me to come over again, right away.

She questioned me about my family once, her face expressionless. She seemed to have developed an interest in her obedient servant.

Cautiously, I started asking about her work, hoping to discover answers from the source of the sickness I needed to treat. She revealed details in dribs and drabs. Often, she cut off the conversation, commanding me to get back to satisfying her lust. Always in control, she prevented me from digging into the contents of her head, contents that I imagined were uglier than her mutilated face. I received her life story in fragments with no leads to follow. Maybe she lied about her past and maybe that wasn't important since our transactions would soon be over anyway. But the scraps themselves kept calling me to piece together a story.

Ariah had apparently been driven to live her life as if it were fiction. She would pass over the denouement – when evil was rooted out in an adventure story, or when the main character found happiness. 'The end of a tale is a compromise,' she said once. 'The middle is a fatty piece of meat, full of gristle, not always easy to chew.'

It seemed that tales first became a driving force in Ariah's life when she was a teenager. Her father had brought an old animated movie about Snow White and her seven dwarf admirers, children. It wasn't the sweet princess who had enthralled her but the Evil Queen who loved only herself. Consumed by jealousy over her stepdaughter, the Evil Queen entered a secret chamber and concocted a deadly potion. Another herb helped her change into a wrinkled old granny. Then she persuaded innocent Snow White to accept the poisoned apple.

Young Ariah had become immersed in this tale in a way that was difficult for me to fathom. In her eyes, the Queen was no mere cruel and jealous woman but a scientist who worked in a spectacular laboratory. Ariah had decided that her own intellect was as sharp as that of the Evil Queen and so had travelled abroad to study. She majored in chemistry and then worked in a research institute at a university until she married.

I pieced together her story based on information that emerged at random, so the tale was incomplete, unsatisfactory. It didn't explain the enigma of her hideousness. Waiting while she bathed one night, I hunted around for further clues. Her room contained a mirror and a dresser. There were no rows of cosmetics. Of course she didn't need beauty products, nothing could redeem her looks. Even the mirror's presence was odd. Why would someone with such a grotesque face want to gaze at herself?

I pulled out a dresser drawer and discovered a stack of documents and a framed picture. I was stunned to see a photo of a beautiful woman around thirty years old with straight black hair. Hair like Ariah's. Could it have been her? If she was so beautiful once, then what had destroyed her face? I began to speculate. Maybe skin cancer had slowly ravaged her until the doctor's verdict had come: she had only a few years to live. She was determined to spend the rest of her life living out her adolescent obsession with freakish tales. She had nothing to lose, not even her place in the world, because she would soon be dead.

When I heard her opening the bathroom door, I quickly shut the drawer. I caught a passing scent of soap, but her rotten smell never disappeared altogether. I returned to the wardrobe, ready to repeat my ritual.

———

My parents always advised me to make safe choices. Prudent calculations pushed me towards a business degree, towards work in an established company, towards selecting an ideal prospective spouse. But now, a month after I signed our contract, Ariah's bedroom had clouded my judgement, had jumbled my perception of security and threat. Her room was a luxury prison. Every time I arrived she took the key from the door and made off with my watch, hiding both as soon as I got into the wardrobe. A long black curtain, thick and motionless, shrouded the room's window. There was no light apart from a harsh blue neon lamp. No wall clock either, so gauging the passage of time was difficult. I didn't know whether she was protecting her secret or hiding her monstrousness from the outside world.

And oh how strange the sights that lay within that room. I, rapist-slave, and Ariah, employer-demon, staring at the ceiling, lighting up a smoke and engaging in pillow talk. We were like two of the damned, ensconced in our cave, shunning the world.

'Did you know,' she said, 'that out there, mothers are protesting about the price of milk?'

Of course I hoped the situation would end soon. Change terrified me. I just wanted to get through all of this and for everything to go back to normal.

She stroked my hair with absurd motherly caresses. Lying beside her, I got used to the sight of her dry lips, pursed half the time, exhaling cigarette smoke. Bathed in the blue glow, her mangled features made me feel as though I was looking at a mermaid who had been dashed against the rocks by the waves. Yet I was shipwrecked, and she was not rescuing me.

At the same time, finding myself so close to a devil summoned a measure of courage. I asked what happened to her face. She thought for a while, then answered, 'It's because I like to experiment.'

She cackled, fixing her gaze on my knitted eyebrows. 'Experiment' apparently was a key word if I wanted to piece together the fragments of her story. A word that I came to regret ever hearing.

When she had first become conscious of her unusual beauty, Ariah had experimented as a chameleon. She had relationships with several men and with each took on the guise of a female stereotype. She became bitchy, pious, shy or indifferent, simply to witness their reactions. Whatever role she chose, her beauty succeeded in swaying men to do anything for her.

One day, as she played the role of a sweet and serious researcher, she met a handsome man at a wedding. They dated for a year and then married. Her new husband asked her to manage a charitable foundation for children. The foundation belonged to his father, a high-ranking official. Ariah left her job at the lab.

Not long after, Ariah discovered that her husband, like most sons of officials, was carrying on relationships with several women. One of them seemed to have become a favourite. Ariah knew the woman: a singer, beautiful, younger than she was. Ariah wanted a divorce but her husband refused, wanting to uphold his reputation. She was a beautiful and intelligent woman, yet she was being kept as a trophy wife. According to her, her husband had been like a gnome incessantly panning for treasure, arranging, collecting. He had been after a wife, a lover and a perfect reputation, all at once.

She spoke as if possessed by her tales. I watched her face grow more and more contorted.

Her comfortable life had begun to feel drab. She frequently returned to the fantasy worlds of her youth. She imagined the Evil Queen, role model for her aborted career as a scientist, venturing into a serpentine underground chamber, coming across her victims' skeletons, crossing rivers at midnight, exploring forests, scrambling over cliffs. The Evil Queen transformed herself into whatever she wanted, beautiful damsel or ugly crone.

In Ariah's formulation, the glamour of experimenting lay in metamorphosis.

She no longer spoke of chameleons, but of butterflies. Not changing clothes, but shedding skin. She had contacted friends from long before and had returned to work in a lab. One night, alone with all those chemicals, she opened a bottle and doused her face with liquid. Her gorgeous features blistered in an instant, corroded beyond recognition.

I shuddered. Not skin cancer – this was even more awful. She wasn't on the verge of death. Not at all.

Ariah had lost consciousness and had been rushed to the hospital. Nobody tried to investigate what had happened. Her husband divorced her shortly afterwards and supplied her with an enormous settlement.

I'd been dragged into a universe of tales so terrible and yet so riveting, I could only gape. I still couldn't fathom what made her destroy herself – divorce, money, boredom?

My sweaty fingers clutched a cigarette until it grew damp. This woman didn't just love tales. She lived them.

'How marvellous,' she said cryptically, 'that the body can be so malleable and change however you want.'

She had a tyrant's arrogance. She celebrated her metamorphosis. And it's not like she had become a butterfly. Then, heightening my alarm, she whispered, 'And, haven't I also managed to capture you?'

———

What could be more terrifying than a devil that speaks truth?

After two months, I still crouched inside the wardrobe, awaiting her. Every morning I hurried to leave the house, playing along with Beauty's game, until we got to a place where she swore, scratched, hurt me. My wife was surprised, even angry, that I was no longer job-hunting, especially when my contract was about to expire.

As for my beautiful wife, who knows what she felt more generally. Of course, thanks to my deal with the devil, we warded off a descent into poverty. But I now allotted more time for work. More precisely, I threw myself into it. I began to avoid my wife for fear that she might notice the scratches and bites on my body. I was Ariah's, so she left marks on me, a slave owner branding her chattel with an iron. I would make love with my wife in the dark. It was excruciating. Another figure forced its way into my head. The incongruous image of a woman with a perfect body and a grotesque face. And – by this point I had lost my mind – I was disappointed when I didn't see that repulsive face and when I wasn't slapped, insulted, degraded. While my body thirsted for that electric shock, shards of that damned story would break off and rearrange themselves in my head.

She had indeed ensnared me, the devil woman. And because she was a real devil, she knew that she had done so. Stroking my back, which was still stinging from the raking of her nails, she said, 'No woman can satisfy you like I do.'

How I hated to hear it, and how right she was. Her next state-ment was more chilling.

'Leave your boring life behind. Come and be an adventurer with me.'

Had she become interested in me, or even fallen in love? Yet her attitude was more like that of a prophet with a new covenant to offer; she wanted to make me her disciple. I felt sick to my stom-ach but couldn't stop to figure out where she wanted to lead me.

Maybe she had made the same offer to the six other men, the slaves who had managed to escape. And she called them failures.

Out of nowhere, bizarre whispers filled my head. The hissing of a demon. *Come with me. Let's run.*

I tensed. These were the temptations of a devil, luring me, testing every weak point. But I bowed my knees in the presence of palpable evil.

'There will never be a dull moment by my side,' she said.

I wasn't sure if I was encountering seduction or disaster, as I felt myself slowly sucked in. I began to imagine what would happen if I left my beautiful wife for this gruesome-looking woman. People would regard me as a corpse that had reappeared from the dead, disturbing the peace as it spread maggots around town. I would be unable to return to my world.

But maybe that would be unnecessary.

These thoughts were so foul that I needed to purge them. I flailed, sought a grip. I tried to revive the whole picture of my past, before I had become captive to this sick tale.

'Experimenting together is such a thrill.'

'What do you mean?'

'We can be a devoted couple and honeymoon in the great cities of the world,' she said. 'Deep down, don't you long to be transformed?'

I looked at her, stunned. She continued slowly, 'I'll make you just as hideous as I am.'

A cold sweat dampened my brow. She wanted to turn me into a monster too. I felt her stories spread through my body, corroding the foundations of my world. My ashen face made her chortle, then she gave me a rough shove. Mounting me, she beat me savagely.

My body didn't react as I hoped. Unable to escape her grip, my addiction to her was obvious. I even begged her to hurt me. Rape me. She shrieked with hysterical laughter and granted my request.

This madness had to come to an end.

With great difficulty, I managed to control my thoughts. Six slaves had understood their plight long before I had, but it wasn't too late. I would quit my job then and there.

Armed with what was left of my sanity, I sought to bargain with the devil. Once our abject lovemaking was over, I sat facing her.

'I can't be with you any more. My wife is pregnant.'

I bowed my face to hide my lie. A whiff of animal odour mixed with blood filled my nostrils. I don't know why but I inhaled that scent deeply.

I calmed my panting and mustered the will to terminate the contract. I promised to pay compensation of a month's wages.

Hearing this, she just smiled ever so faintly. But the disgusting boils on her face hardened and I thought I could spy evil in her eyes.

'All right,' she said. 'Tomorrow is your last day of work.'

———

I shouldn't have come. But some impulse had made me want to see her one last time. Like a junkie, I thought. A ritual of closure before I straightened out. A farewell of sorts to the depravity that had seduced me, which I would taste no more. The end of any story is a compromise, as she had once said.

I crouched there in the wardrobe, waiting for her, counting my heartbeats before I could finally pounce. Then I heard a heavy click. The wardrobe doors were being locked.

I called her name, hesitant, not daring to guess what was happening. She didn't answer. My calls grew increasingly urgent, then turned into screams. This was no time to joke. Or to experiment.

The hair on the back of my neck bristled as that evil word reverberated in my head. I pounded on the solid teak. When that didn't work I heaved against the door. It was all in vain. My rape uniform was drenched in sweat. I caught the stench of her presence. Then another smell invaded the closed space: my own piss, uncontrollable, flooding my underwear.

Who knows how many hours or days I've been in here now. She has robbed me of anything that might mark time. While it flows on as usual outside the room, I am trapped in here. A slow murder.

I no longer attempt to escape. I slump into my own shit. A new piece of Ariah's story slots into place. Perhaps the six men before me didn't escape either. How stupid of me never to wonder where they had ended up. Perhaps all of them were addicted like me, even on their day of repentance, surrendering themselves to her fatal experiments. And this is where we have all ended up: in the dark.

I crouch in this clammy and suffocating enclosure, imagining her out there, laughing scornfully, revelling in her hideous face. A pocked face that invites the mirth of maggots. Rotting. Bewitching.

The Well

**'I won't be home too late.'**

'I wind up in pain when you come back late. A lot of pain.'

'Yes, Pa. I know. See you later, Pa.'

Dahlia, the youngest daughter, cared for her sickly father. Her siblings survived on her blood, leeches that they were. Their right to movement, procreation, business, labour and leisure – all of it depended on Dahlia's existence. Beloved daughter, Pa's little girl, youngest sister to all the siblings. She was the last born, frequently overlooked. And see how powerless he had become: he whose voice had once boomed through the halls of the household, he who could ferret out the trembling lies of his children as they cowered under the table, a tyrant who wielded an iron fist in the name of love. Now he was merely a pensioner. His grey hair stank of pomade and he was helpless without his afternoon nap. His 78-year-old heart was weak and he was so dependent on his daughter that he had a constant need to grasp her hand.

'Your grip's too tight, Pa.'

'Don't leave me.'

*Do you depend on me, or do you refuse to let me go because I'm a brittle hair, easily uprooted from your scalp and swept away? Are you afraid of losing me?*

Dahlia was her father's favourite. Her siblings knew this. When she finished her schooling in the mediocre little town where they lived, they asked her to put off finding a job, to take care of the old man. The former authoritarian hated nursemaids and only wanted his beloved daughter. *Come on, he won't live long.* Her siblings shared the burden of financial support, and two years ago she, formally a princess, joined the ranks of the unemployed.

They bought her a wide-screen TV so she wouldn't get bored. She never complained, even though she couldn't go out with her friends much, or date. Besides, no suitor had come into her life. Of all the many knights, as yet none had had sufficient vigour to vanquish the father.

'Men of today are losers unworthy of my daughter.'

The old man didn't care that his youngest child might hold a different opinion.

In the house there was only the father and daughter, the daughter's cats and a maid who went home for the afternoon. It was a magnificent house for a small town, inherited from his grandfather, the father of the previous ruler. Ah, he too wielded power; a regent who spent his youth drinking wine with colonial officials. His legacy was a Dutch-era house with a faded terrazzo floor. It had a large storehouse and a deep well. There were many doors. Closed, of course. A symbol of the ancestral kingdom.

One door among them was special to Dahlia, a red door near the storehouse in the darkest corner. Above the door hung cobwebs.

There was a deep secret between Dahlia and the door that she hadn't divulged to her father or any of her siblings.

One day, she had opened the red door and stepped into a forest. Yes, truly. A forest. She clung tightly to this enormous secret. In the scorching heat of the afternoon – when she couldn't stomach another TV show or munching her slothful way through yet another bag of potato crisps; when she wearied of her lonely home, far from the gleam of myriad neon lights; or when she was simply sick and tired of every damn thing – Dahlia would sneak into the woods. When she felt a tightness in her chest, the forest offered her plenty of air. Several times, she returned from an excursion on the other side of the door, barely suppressing an urge to scream. Out of fear, out of happiness, out of anger – maybe all three. Anything at all, just not boredom.

Behind the red door, a new world revealed itself to her. Not far from it stood an old, moss-covered well. She peered into it and felt something like an electric shock jolting her out of a century-long slumber. The water in the well was clear and calm but a shadow had appeared on it. The shadow of a face. No. She shuddered. Not a face. There was only a head and eye sockets, holes that led down to the darkest depths. The face had no features; all was emptiness and two holes, ending who knows where.

Dahlia tried to tear her eyes away, her heart racing.

She experienced a feeling more unsettling than horror. A sense of wanting to reach out to the emptiness, to lose herself within it. As she tried to look away, the shadow grew more distinct. Dahlia could make out the creature, from the waist up to the neck. The figure was naked with long, dishevelled hair and breasts. A woman.

But who? Who was this faceless woman, whose eyes dropped away to nothingness?

Dahlia now realised that the shadow followed all her movements. When she touched the water with her right hand, the woman extended her left. As she tilted her head back, those deep eyes vanished. Don't – Don't look away. *My mirror.*

From that moment on, something behind the red door had transformed itself. Was it the well or the forest? Dahlia wasn't sure but she always came to stare at the shadow. The mirror in her room now seemed to throng with nauseating lies. That dulled glass had become a director of cheap horror films with cheesy but creepy special effects. She hated the face in it. She didn't want to have a face. Only eyes. Yes, eyes that could see everything. Like the eyes of the woman in the well.

*Had someone else also been peering into the well?*

The well obsessed her, even after she returned to the outside world. She felt estranged from that world, above all from the body she didn't want to possess. As she walked the streets in the crowd, her worn-out frame always felt like it was moving against her will. Her body and mind had undergone a separation but even so it was her body, rather than her mind, that remained a concern for those around her. Wrinkles, stretch marks, skin folds, varicose veins, pores the size of potholes. People in her world were crazy about putting these flaws under a microscope, simply for the relief at not suffering from them.

Come Friday night, her friends went out on dates. So did Dahlia. After her father had gone to sleep, she had her own enthralling tryst with what lay beyond the red door.

Sometimes she wanted to step through and never return.

———

'Do you remember how naughty Adit was?'

A bedtime ritual. Dahlia sat next to Pa, accompanying him as he wandered among sepia-toned memories. A melancholic nostalgia that she knew by heart.

'Do you remember when he set his report card on fire? He didn't dare come home until late at night. Your mum and I were worried sick until a neighbour finally brought him back. He arrived in filthy clothes – only the devil knows what he'd been up to – and his face was all sulky. Did he think he could just come and go like a hotel?'

Dahlia remembered her father's wrath. He whipped Adit with a belt. Twice.

'I might have been a little hard on him,' her father admitted. 'But look at the fruits of my discipline now. Just look at the man Adit has become.'

A respectable lawyer, one of Dahlia's key benefactors.

'And Rama. He wouldn't have a job at a multinational now if I'd let him keep wasting his time with that amateur band of his.'

Then Sarita, Dahlia recalled.

She wasn't allowed to utter that forbidden name. Sarita, Sarita. Sarita, who smoked marijuana. Sarita, who slept with the son of her father's friend. Sarita, who ran away overseas with her beloved.

Secretly, Sarita financially supported Dahlia, too.

'But you, my little girl, you are the best. Even when you were a baby, you hardly cried, and you were always very obedient,' he patted Dahlia's head, as if stroking a bunny.

Lulled by his reminiscences, the old man drifted off to sleep. Dahlia watched his eyes close. Night paves the way for little princesses to engage in their petty betrayals.

*For everything that I cannot do like Adit, Rama and Sarita.*

Dahlia moved away from her father and tiptoed towards the red door.

She pressed down on its carved handle. The door creaked open. Air surged from behind it, carrying not the stale smell of dust that had settled indoors for too long, but the fresh moisture of dew that formed on leaves at night. Rather than the hardness of the floor, her feet now trod on soft, cold grass. Here was a forest and above it a black sky topped by an eternal rainbow. Crimson, chocolate and indigo blended as beautifully as a gaping wound. Her alternate world – the world behind the door, where the owl never sleeps and the rustling branches create a language of their own.

*Ah, welcome back to our forest, child of humankind. Soon the celebration will begin. Look, they have gathered around the campfire.*

She hadn't known of life in the forest. A group of men and women as beautiful as fairies smiled at her. Plant tendrils, twisting like snakes, supplied their clothing.

*Come, come, sit here.*

She wanted to know what it felt like to be one of them. To dance to music she had never heard, partake of the most mouth-watering fruits, wear a constant smile. But she was reluctant to join – it was as though they spoke a different tongue. Dahlia settled herself on a rock not far away, admiring the festivities.

All of a sudden, she felt the ground beneath her tremble and then crack. She looked at the dancers. Had their frolicking caused it? No, no; they didn't seem to notice. Something was amiss. Careful to avoid drawing anyone's attention, she withdrew slowly and hid behind a tree. Yes, something was amiss. And whatever that something was felt very close.

Slowly, the glow of the campfire dimmed then disappeared entirely, swallowed by an enormous shadow. Dahlia squinted, trying to peer at the danger that was taking shape. A wolf, but far too huge for an ordinary wolf. It was as tall as a tree.

A giant wolf wanted to join the merrymaking and the beautiful creatures realised it too late. The wolf approached the festive crowd, hurled them into the air, lunged at their necks. Dahlia covered her mouth. She was witnessing a massacre. Blood flowed from shredded flesh but the faces retained their smiles.

Beautiful heads were liberated from bodies. They sprawled behind the leaves, were flung to the treetops, bounced along the paths. Perfect faces that smiled until death.

Now she doubted whether they were ever alive.

Dahlia dared not leave her hiding place. Silence had taken hold of the night. The screaming had stopped. All were dead.

The giant wolf, however, remained. It began to sniff out Dahlia, the only being left from the massacre. The night was so still. The only sounds were her breath and that of the wolf. The eyes of the great beast cast around. Dahlia retreated slowly. She tried to recall where the red door was.

She would run to it, open it, then slam it shut, never to return.

There had to be something that would distract the wolf. She wished another creature in the thicket would arouse the monster's desire, so she could run as fast as she could. But the party had ended. Only she and the predator were left.

Dahlia remembered an old trick, her last hope. Yes, she would throw a pebble as far as possible. Then she would dart away.

One.

Her fingers trembled as she picked up a pebble. Careful, careful.

Two.

Grasping the pebble, she waited a moment. She would have to be swift and precise.

Now was the time.

Three!

She threw the pebble and sprinted away with all the speed she could muster.

Over ditches and barbed hedges. The grasses were like wildfire that singed and stung her legs. Soon... soon a door would appear.

The door was near the well.

But which one? She found one well, then another, and another. She had to find the well that reflected the shadow of a woman with deep eyes.

Her knees had gone numb but she kept running. The wolf's fury could be felt so near, its breath on her ears. Soon. Soon there will be...

A red door... No door!

The door wasn't there. She had merely circled back to her starting point. Here was where the party had been. Here, too, the party had ended. She couldn't escape; the master of the house liked her scent.

She whirled around. The wolf loomed in front of her, its eyes full of embers and boring into her. Its fangs glittered.

At that moment came the sensation. A comet that had flown off for just a fraction of a second and made her gasp. The feeling when a car almost skids off into a ravine on a sharp curve. Resisting. Crashing. Eyes closing. But then—

Release.

Surrendering to the darkness, she saw a hand reaching for her. The woman of the well with infinite eyes. She drove the wolf away with a mere swish of the hand then took Dahlia and flew into the well.

Now she understood everything. The well was a sea of red wine.

Blood blackening boiling billowing.

Unfolding the origins of life.

And death.

The woman invited her—

to haunt eternally the boundless deep.

Yes.

Let's do that.

*Pa, Pa ... See you later. Tomorrow I won't be late. Goodnight, Pa.*

They will meet again tomorrow at sunrise.

If she wakes up.

*If.*

**Salimah twisted, sweaty and sinuous, bathed in the colourful** lights. In skin-tight leggings and a beaded, black dress that hardly concealed her voluptuous curves, she swayed to the beat. Her cat-like eyes were framed by false lashes. They looked straight at the audience. The men, bewitched, swore to drop to their knees and surrender to the curve of her hips and to lavish kisses on her shiny black stiletto boots. Her mouth, rimmed with scarlet Viva lipstick, opened as she encouraged the crowd to dance.

No question about it, her killer moves made men obsessed.

The villagers adored a few other dangdut singers besides Salimah, like Tety Maryaty and Cici Ciara. They were equally skilled and had a similar pedigree: each had participated in the selection for festivals for Qu'ranic readings and each had dreamed of becoming a pop singer before finally joining the Red Honey Dangdut Band. Tety Maryaty was never seen out of her tufted shirt and leopard print pants; she was a bit too curvaceous to carry off the sporty look she so wished to emulate. Cici Ciara, on the other hand, tended towards a wistful expression and dreamy eyes; she could turn any song into something melancholy.

Unlike her peers, Salimah was never too peppy or too woeful. Her singing was dynamic. It was crisp and untamed. She called to mind Elvy Sukaesih, the Queen of Dangdut. Salimah's movements were graceful, seductive, sometimes passionate. But she always seemed to be holding something back. It was as if her dress, which barely left her room to breathe, was keeping an enormous power in check. Many said the gleam in her eyes resembled Itje Trisnawati's. But unlike Itje, who acted coquettishly, Salimah was never known to play around. Far from feeling discomforted by a man's gaze, she relished it. And then crushed it. Her eyes inflicted a sting, as if she were constantly searching for something. Loyal fans fantasised about what she would be like if she ever let loose the fire she guarded within.

The women who grew up with Salimah knew she was older than she looked. They tracked her life history: married at seventeen; a mother a year later; divorced at twenty-three; single until now, age thirty. For a village dangdut singer, she wasn't all that young.

Surely she had inserted a susuk into the soft tissue of her body as a talisman. That, at least, is what her neighbours whispered. There was something mesmerising in her allure and some found this terrifying. Not a few were convinced that Salimah had turned to magic, that she had made a dark sacrifice, probably a life, for her beauty. But her fans didn't care. Sexy widow or the reincarnation of Nini Pelet, complete with her love potions, the woman was a knockout.

'Is this addictive or what?' Salimah shouted in the microphone. 'Let's see you move!'

Salimah's voice reverberated even after the concert. The night market had already dispersed but, cradling cheap liquor, men were still jabbering about how she moved.

'Who would you go for, Cici or Salimah? A girl, or a lady with experience?'

'As if you know the difference.'

'Salimah has such a great butt, she must work it around in bed.'

It wasn't just the drunks who daydreamed about Salimah. Innocent youth and upstanding husbands did, too. They showered her with small gifts. A kid or two would look for her backstage, where the ladies changed in a makeshift cubicle that was overflowing with cosmetics and costumes, speckled with snack crumbs and heady with the scent of deodorant. The boys, harmless enough to trespass on this female domain, delivered gifts from Salimah's fans.

'Hey, Miss Salimah, somebody bought you martabak. Here.'

'Who?'

'Same as usual, Solihin.'

Salimah thought back to how so many teenage girls, herself included, would steal glances at Solihin when he was on his way to the mosque. Salimah was certain that he gazed back at her, but for years he never dared make a move and he ended up marrying another woman instead. He was struggling for recognition in the community and courting Salimah wouldn't help. Besides, he thought that Salimah would only be interested in rich men, who would spoil her with expensive dresses but never offer to marry her. Now, even after sending her several gifts, Solihin pretended not to notice when Salimah smiled at him in the street.

The slightly cracked and clouded mirror reflected Salimah's make-up-free face. She was busily trimming her eyebrows with a pair of clippers. Whether or not she had the help of a charm, half an hour later that mirror revealed an enchantress.

Salimah left the martabak untouched. She passed it on to the band, so they would have a snack when they finished performing.

Salimah sometimes invited men on stage to dance with her. Now and then a man would take the opportunity to snuggle up to her and peek at her cleavage, or even try to kiss her on the cheek. Fans who overstepped their bounds got a shove from Salimah but, still, she smiled and her eyes twinkled mischievously as she sang. 'So many times, I've played around with love...'

Salimah's reputation as a dangdut queen lasted until at least the mid-nineties. That's when things changed. More and more villagers proclaimed themselves pious. They gathered in the mosque and zealously denounced those addicted to dangdut or, more precisely, addicted to Salimah's provocative gyrations. The loudest protests came from Haji Ahmad, a local authority. Previously, he'd seemed unperturbed by her presence. Even his wife regularly chatted with Salimah after Tarawih prayers during Ramadan. Now, Haji Ahmad said, 'The provocative dancing of dangdut bringeth only evil. No good can come of it. Guard thyselves, O my fellow Muslims, from immorality, from liquor, and from accursed women.'

His condemnation grew. 'And indeed, how great the distance between sight and sound. It is not dangdut that is sinful, but intoxicating women, who arouse lust. Such women are the root of fornication, of zina. The zina that we often fail to notice, O Muslim brothers and sisters, is the adultery of the eyes.'

Haji Ahmad believed dangdut as a musical form could be redeemed, as when the king of the genre, Rhoma Irama, preached through song. He still remembered when Rhoma, now a haji, visited the village. It was several years ago, before Suharto's fall. The former president's party, Golkar, was campaigning in the village.

Although Haji Ahmad couldn't forgive Rhoma for abandoning his struggle on behalf of an Islamic political party, the shrill singing of the lord of dangdut met with his firm approval:

'Emancipation of women, do not oppose the will of God, this is calaaaaaamity...'

'Amen.'

'O ye women, keep thine honour!'

Now it wasn't the wail of Rhoma that could be heard but the voice of Haji Ahmad reverberating through mosque loudspeakers: 'For too long, the people's morals have been allowed to go to ruin. Look at what our children watch on television. All manner of Western influence. All manner of unseemly nakedness. All manner of decadence. Let us engage in moral jihad!'

His rage reached its peak during the Independence Day celebrations. Nothing truly unprecedented transpired but the incident took place in broad daylight, when the sun made everything more shameful. A man clambered onto the stage to dance with Salimah. Although he only jerked his thumbs around while barely moving his hips, his eyes were unblinking, staring at Salimah's shoulders and the motion of her hips as she shimmied.

Suddenly, a shout from the audience: 'Hey! He's got a hard-on!'

Others repeated the cry and some hooted. The audience was in a half-mocking, half-jealous uproar. At the song's end, shouts thundered forth, accompanying the man's descent from the stage. Salimah continued her singing but that afternoon everyone's head carried a vivid set of pictures: Salimah's curves, a lustful male gaze and a physical reaction witnessed by all.

News about the man's arousal on stage spread quickly. Haji Ahmad's wrath could no longer be restrained. Here was proof of zina of the eye. Salimah's dancing was toxic.

'We must oppose Salimah's immorality to the death!'

The following day, after the festivities subsided, a group of men confronted Salimah in her home. The delegation claimed to be acting on behalf of a mosque and was led by Haji Ahmad. But Salimah, who spent her teen years at a mosque, knew full well that several of the men were anything but devout. She had seen them gambling and selling downers in dim street stalls. But maybe the situation really had changed. Haji Ahmad forbade Salimah from singing again. If she did, she would have to leave the village. Salimah saw anger boiling in his eyes, eyes that for many years had held a different radiance.

——

Trivialities tend to evaporate from memory but Salimah never forgot. She remembered when Haji Ahmad came to the mosque, replacing Haji Ibrahim, to teach Qur'anic recitation to the youth. He lectured teenage girls, subjugating their thinking. At that point Salimah, only fourteen, dared not look any man in the eye. She wouldn't meet the gaze of her recitation teacher, though she surreptitiously observed how Haji Ahmad, who was in his early forties, was much more handsome than elderly Haji Ibrahim or even Solihin, who all the village girls were crazy about.

One night, Salimah was the last student at the mosque. Haji Ahmad asked her to work through a segment of the Holy Book, to determine her readiness for a Qur'anic reading contest. They sat facing each other. Salimah read the Sūrat an-Nūr, with its prescriptions on morality. After a few verses, Salimah realised that Haji Ahmad wasn't paying attention. She made deliberate mistakes but her teacher didn't correct her. Salimah sensed Haji Ahmad leaning further forward until his breathing caught her attention. Heavy breath. Masculine breath. Salimah raised her head.

Haji Ahmad was staring at her. His eyes held an odd, ambiguous look, as if they could penetrate her veil and the shirt buttoned up to her neck. Salimah met his gaze. They stared at each other for a long time until footsteps could be heard approaching the door. The muezzin of the mosque.

The next day, Haji Ahmad acted as if nothing had happened. Salimah felt disappointed, though she wasn't sure why. To be more precise, she didn't want to know why. For several years after that, she was conscious of Haji Ahmad staring at her from afar while she pretended to look down. Salimah tried to guess what might have happened if the muezzin hadn't appeared. Each time she did, anger rose within her. Her cheeks flushed and her heart beat fast. Maybe Haji Ahmad had gone senile. But even now, after tormenting several pairs of eyes with her body and her own glances, Salimah never forgot that he was the one who had taught her how dangerous the gaze can be.

———

After the Independence Day incident, Salimah, dangdut queen who aroused the village men, never received another invitation to perform. The fans who had revered her didn't defend her in the least, though they still ogled her and whistled when she passed.

'Hey, Sal, when do I get my dance?'

'Salimah, Salimah, Salome has a hole where all of us can play!'

Salimah stopped and glared. Furious, she scooped up a handful of gravel, ready to pelt the shameless mouths before her.

'You dog!' she retorted. 'All you'll ever get hold of is your own dick!'

One day, Salimah left the village without so much as a word of goodbye. Asep, her son, stayed behind, looking after a neighbour's roadside stall. Whenever he was asked about his mother, he simply replied that she was working elsewhere. Her name came up occasionally, when the villagers reminisced about her seductive swaying and how it had obsessed the men.

Two years later, a woman with a hijab and a haggard face appeared in the village one quiet night. Almost nobody recognised her. Salimah. A dull white headscarf framed a face caked in cheap, chalky powder and blotchy red lipstick. The villagers were unsure whether her lips were smiling or grimacing in pain.

People began to concoct their own versions of how Salimah came to be the way she was now. Some said she had been whoring in the village before she left, had contracted a filthy disease and had then looked for a job in the city so she could treat it. Other rumours told of how she had been a migrant worker in Malaysia until her employer beat her. Whatever the reason, she had changed. With that headscarf in place, Salimah looked more subdued. But she didn't seem to be going through rebirth as a pious Muslim. She had returned in a state of ruin. She glowered at everyone around her.

She was no longer a shapely dangdut queen but a terrifying, strange woman. None of her former fans dared approach her, except one.

That fan was Solihin, who used to lavish her with gifts. Not long ago, he had been appointed village head. Previously, Solihin had memorised the songs that Salimah crooned. He became intimate with her rhythms and sighs, calculating to the second when she would perform her signature moves. He gawked when she wiped away her sweat or got too hot and undid her jacket, revealing bare shoulders that sparkled in the lights. Salimah now looked strange, even creepy. She was no longer an object of fantasy, no longer capable of making anyone obsess over her.

He asked Salimah to become his second wife, unofficially. The power he now wielded allowed him everything he always wanted but couldn't have. Only Salimah had escaped him. To his astonishment, she refused. If she had rejected him ten years before, perhaps he wouldn't have been devastated. But now was different. He was a village head and Salimah was no longer a dangdut queen. Was his offer not an act of compassion, as when the Prophet had married middle-aged widows?

Clear images of the former Salimah hovered before Solihin's eyes, disconcerting him. While making love to his wife, Solihin saw Salimah's red lips. But reality can't keep up its deceptions indefinitely. His wife's hips were not those of Salimah, whose sensuous thrusts had so bewitched him. Solihin had never in his life been known to be wild or to gamble or drink. Yet, being addicted to a widow was more dangerous.

Battling to conceal his desperation, he made a new offer. If Salimah wouldn't be his wife, then Solihin wanted to see her as she used to be, when she captivated men, when the succulence of her body and her sighs haunted his wickedest imaginings.

The village head wanted Salimah to dance for him and for that he was prepared to give whatever she asked.

'You only want me to dance?' asked Salimah in disbelief.

Solihin paused. Then, in a low voice, muffling his lust, his anger and his disappointment, he said, 'I want to watch you strip as you move.'

Solihin tried to meet Salimah's eyes without blinking but her gaze, no less piercing than when she sang all those years ago, challenged his pride. He licked his parched lips. Salimah burst into savage, mocking laughter.

'If that's what you want, then it's an expensive gift I'm after.'

'Money isn't a problem,' said Solihin, impatient but trying to protect his dignity. 'Do you want a motorbike? I hear Asep wants to drive a motorcycle taxi.'

Salimah shook her head.

'A house?'

When he let those words escape, Solihin realised he was gambling. He had gone too far. He felt an uncontrollable surge of lust. Salimah shook her head firmly. She pressed against Solihin and whispered slowly in his ear.

Solihin was aghast. His knees went weak.

Salimah's loyal fans knew that she never joked. She played for keeps.

Solihin caught vengeance in her eyes, tired eyes that no longer gleamed like those of a cat. Circumstances had changed but Salimah still stoked a fire deep within him. He would fight to get the woman he had struggled to win years before.

———

Solihin had developed and perfected his master plan. Tonight was the night. He had paid neighbourhood thugs to intercept Haji Ahmad on his way home after evening prayers. Familiar faces. Some had been among those who accused Salimah and forbade her dancing. Solihin had never before hired thugs on account of a woman.

It wasn't hard to shadow Haji Ahmad. Everybody knew his habits; he wouldn't set out until the rest of the congregation had left the mosque. Solihin's minions dragged him from the main road to a deserted alley. He put up a fight.

At one in the morning, Solihin picked up Salimah. With no time to dress, Salimah wore only a negligee, adding a leather jacket as protection against the night breeze. She also had on a rumpled headscarf. Solihin drove his motorbike towards an area covered in scrub that people rarely passed through, a place where evil spirits brought death to infants. Occasionally, he gazed at the sky. How strange the moon was that night.

In the bushes, Solihin set down a black plastic bag beside Salimah, not saying a word. She stared at the pale face of her devotee, then shifted her gaze towards the dowry she had demanded. Carefully, she knelt, patting the plastic surface, weighing it. Damp. Heavy. She took a long look inside to confirm that Solihin had kept his promise.

'Put on the music,' Salimah's voice was icy.

Solihin had made sure the batteries in the cassette player were charged. Setting it on the ground, he played a song that Salimah always sang when she performed, a song that made him fall in love over and over; a song that resounded as, in his dreams, the woman, damp with perspiration, ran her hands all over him.

Salimah loosened her headscarf. She tossed her jacket towards Solihin and began moving to the rhythm of the music. Solihin bathed the object of his worship in the beam of his torch, trying to recall how the stage lights had bathed her. There was always something elusive about her. A pent-up passion, reserved for who knows what. Salimah raised the tip of her negligee, past her knee, past her thigh, then higher and higher still until Solihin glimpsed her famed hips. The woman twisted slowly, biting her lips, not taking her eyes off Solihin. Salimah's body was withered, emaciated, but in the eyes of Solihin she hadn't changed at all. His heart pounded so hard he thought he might die.

Her negligee had now fallen to the ground. His goddess shimmied, moving back towards the plastic bag. Solihin was drained and shaking. Salimah lifted the offering he had made to her. The head of Haji Ahmad.

Yet what she had long desired was not his head, but his eyes. The eyes of Haji Ahmad were open wide, just as when he had gazed at Salimah while she read the Sūrat an-Nūr, just as when he had declared her a source of sin. Salimah stared and stared at the eyes before her, stroking the lids. Her fingers trembled. Though the past resurfaced in her memories, it never repeated itself as it should have.

Like a child who has found a lost doll, Salimah cradled the head of Haji Ahmad against her chest. Drops of blood fell on her. Salimah's eyes were tearful, shut. Her lips were half open. Moist.

No longer able to maintain his strength, Solihin dropped to his knees. His heart felt as if it would stop as he witnessed the morass of desire and grief in front of him. The throbbing of death and passion, exposed. The moon was naked, the night was damp.

Everything else happened swiftly. The sound of approaching clapper sticks grew louder. The villagers surrounded Solihin and Salimah, and beat them without mercy. Their blood had now been sanctioned as halal.

Seriously wounded, Solihin was dragged to the police station. Salimah didn't survive. The rage of the mob flared at the sight of the woman hugging the head of Haji Ahmad, her body smeared with gore. Her snarled hair and wild eyes made the villagers' blood boil. Clubs struck her again and again. She collapsed, thrashed relentlessly, but still her hands clutched the head. Some compassionate members of the mob closed its bulging eyes. The killing moon was pale, cold and bare.

This tragic story has been passed on and framed carefully. The beginning of destruction was a sin that we often don't recognise: zina of the eyes. Salimah was condemned and her life endlessly discussed. Everyone remembers her in different ways. Some night, when you are strolling about in the village, cast your gaze to the sky. If the moon looks strange, like a woman who has risen from the grave, you'll know that she has never departed.

# The Porcelain Doll

There were no obvious changes after the red-cheeked porcelain doll shattered. The house stayed an old house, well maintained. It was kept clean and tidy to distract visitors' attention from all the leaks. Though it wasn't overly big, Grandpa hadn't raised enough money to repair it.

Grandma didn't want the neighbours to know that they were short of cash to renovate the inherited home so she put effort into making it beautiful. Every day she checked to see if the flower-embroidered tablecloth had any stains, if the terrazzo tiles needed dusting, if the jar in the living room was still stocked with simple pastries. Sweetie still ate from her bowl. Rice and fish.

The shattering of the porcelain doll didn't change the world.

Grandma still paid careful attention to her daily routine. Brewing hot beverages in the morning. Black coffee for Grandpa and tea for herself. As she stirred, she gazed at the thick coffee.

Steaming and lustrous. But something always settled at the bottom. Something dark, black and clotting.

Grandma continued to pour creativity into their meals. They were never extravagant, but she varied them every two days. Only now she needed more time. To knead the dough. To scrutinise every grain of salt. After cooking she would scrub the soiled dishes thoroughly and then rinse them at full pressure until they squeaked. There was dirt that couldn't be seen, bacteria that survived despite repeated sanitising.

Meanwhile, Grandpa still took his breakfast while reading the newspaper. Just like in elementary school primers. He spent afternoons in his study. Since retiring he liked to read a lot, especially about successful celebrities (particularly former officials or generals), treatises on alternative medicine and books about plants. He used to raise an eclectic array of plants in his small yard. But gardening requires a fair bit of money so he wasn't as active as he used to be. Still, he tended the plants in the knowledge that something cared for in the nursery would not take its leave when it matured.

Grandpa still sat there, at the dining table covered in plastic to protect the tablecloth, sipping coffee and peering at the world as it was presented in the morning newspaper. He would peruse the paper from first page to last and then return to the first page. When she passed by, Grandma would offer, 'Fried banana?' He would nod. Then she would get back to bustling about as queen of her little fiefdom, in the kitchen, and he would continue reading, his mouth closed. At lunch, she would say, 'Eat up, the food will get cold.' 'Yes, yes,' he would respond automatically. He dined alone because she had eaten beforehand in the kitchen. As a queen, she could take her repast whenever and wherever she liked.

Day and night came and went, the elderly couple repeating the same sentences. Sometimes there were slight variations, such as when Grandpa sat on the couch watching the news on television.

'Wow. Petrol has gone up again. Lucky we only have a motorbike.'

Grandma, busy filling a jar with roasted peanuts, responded without tilting her head, 'What isn't getting more expensive these days?'

In the late afternoon she would tidy up old magazines – editions of *Kartini* from a dozen years ago – so that they kept their slick look under the table. At that hour she would turn on the television, the volume loud, to listen to a celebrity gossip show without having to turn.

'So, she finally got divorced too,' commented Grandma about a celebrity now and then. How wonderful that magic box was, saving them from ever feeling alone.

Grandpa went to bed early. Grandma, as appropriate for a monarch, would not retire until she had inspected her realm and its subjects: tables, chairs, pots, vases.

They lived as before, now without the red-cheeked porcelain doll.

Previously, the beautiful figurine had stood atop an antique wooden chest from Bali. The chest was placed in the living room as a centrepiece. On it they put souvenirs from abroad. A model windmill from Holland, an engraved cup from Thailand and Yin Yin, the porcelain doll with rosy cheeks from China.

The windmill was a gift from a former boss of Grandpa's who frequently went abroad. Music sounded when the blades turned. The cup had been given by neighbours – fellow pensioners, but with many children, one of whom worked in a travel agency. Their house could no longer accommodate all the mementoes from different countries. Grandpa assumed the neighbour kept giving them only to show off, but Grandma gratefully accepted a cup that could embellish their home.

As for Yin Yin, she was a gift from their nephew, Ardi. When Ardi was small, his mother, Grandpa's younger sister, was so busy that Ardi was often deposited with the childless couple. Ardi had never forgotten Grandma and Grandpa's kindness and often stopped by with keepsakes.

Yin Yin was the best. Her fingers were delicate, dainty. Perhaps equally as beautiful as her bound feet – small, white, immaculate. Beautiful. Fragile.

Anyone would admire her beauty. The doll had tiny almond eyes. Smooth skin, rosy cheeks, heart-shaped lips. Her smile was so sweet that Grandpa and Grandma never sought comparisons. A perfect smile. A porcelain smile.

But one day, Grandma discovered Yin Yin toppled from the antique chest. She was shattered in pieces. And so was Grandma.

Sweetie was the culprit. Cats are ingrates.

Near the chest, Grandma spotted woollen yarn, a plaything of Sweetie's. She must have been trying to make off with it so eagerly that Yin Yin became a casualty. Cats are the same everywhere.

What cut Grandma and Grandpa to the quick was the fact that Yin Yin was shattered. If she'd been stolen, maybe they wouldn't have been wounded so deeply. At least her body would have remained intact. Perhaps someone rich would have bought her from the thief and she could have decorated a mansion with marble floors. At least that would have been more comforting than to see her violated, ruined, destroyed. Grandma found her lying decapitated on the floor, her pretty little feet in their velvet shoes detached from the body.

Grandpa tried to glue Yin Yin together again. The worst part was the doll's torso. It had shattered into too many fragments to reattach them all and he was unable to fill a large cavity on Yin Yin's back. After the sections of her body were reconnected, the figurine was returned to its position. But Grandma's expression grew more wistful. Yin Yin's beauty looked artificial. Her wounds left her with a rough, ugly scar on her neck. Anyone who flipped her around would discover a crater in Yin Yin's back.

The red-cheeked porcelain doll had been transformed into Sundel Bolong, the prostitute of legend, the ghost with a hole in her back. And so she was taken down from the chest and shut away in a drawer. They locked it tight. The darkness is long for those who are not whole.

---

The cat was initially called Sweetie. Not because names for cats in the area were limited to Sweetie, Kitty, Puss and the like but because she acted sweeter than her mother, Bandit. Bandit had earned her name after wandering off for days and swiping a fish from Grandma's kitchen as soon as she returned. But Grandma did not chase her away. They needed a cat; the old house was plagued with mice. Besides, cats were beloved by the Prophet.

Bandit gave birth in the house. Like all cats, she was shameless: she'd been impregnated by a dozen toms over the years. When she mated the racket was deafening. Grandma was used to being disturbed by the caterwauling of coupling felines but she had never heard wilder, fiercer howls than Bandit's. A cheap whore. Her offspring were scattered everywhere. God knows how many of Bandit's kittens Grandma had given away to neighbourhood kids. But Sweetie looked so funny at birth with the trio of stripes on her body. White, yellow, black. People said that calico cats brought good luck. Grandma and Grandpa both wanted to keep her.

Sweetie turned out to be far sweeter than her mother, perhaps because she had been trained in the niceties of human civilisation from kittenhood. She faithfully carried out her duty of catching mice. She knew where to relieve herself, although Grandma from time to time had to clean up her poo outside the bathroom door. Annoying, but forgivable. We can't expect a cat to be too perfect, can we?

But after the tragic shattering of Yin Yin, Sweetie encountered bitter treatment. Every time she wandered onto the terrace or into the kitchen, it was as if a placard had been hung around her neck, saying:

| | |
|---|---|
| NAME: | SWEETIE |
| AGE: | 2½ YEARS |
| CHARGE: | WILFULLY TOPPLING YIN YIN, PORCELAIN DOLL, FROM HER PLACE OF SANCTUARY. |
| VERDICT: | GUILTY |

For a cat whose motives carried a whiff of vandalism, there was no more fitting sentence than banishment.

After the porcelain doll with the red cheeks shattered, Sweetie still ate from her old plate. Her rations of rice and fish weren't reduced. But the elderly couple never greeted her again. Sweetie felt numb, unable to taste the fish. Grandma's gaze was so bitter and venomous that Sweetie wanted to swallow her own tongue.

———

Ardi visited several months after the incident. He had just returned from a tour of several countries in Asia. He gave Grandma a box, gift-wrapped with a pretty ribbon. She, of course, opened it joyfully. But, after all this time, her smile appeared feigned. How surprised she was to find her gift: a male figurine in traditional Chinese costume, crimson, festive and opulent. He was the same size as Yin Yin.

'A perfect match for Yin Yin, isn't he?'

Grandma regarded the doll for a long time. Very good, she thought. How fine a partner for Yin Yin. If. Supposing.

Oh, dear... this prince would not take pleasure in a damaged bride. She and Grandpa looked at each other, sharing silent disappointment.

Seeing the smile vanish from his aunt's face, Ardi asked what the matter was. With a heavy heart, Grandma recounted how the porcelain doll had tumbled from the antique chest.

'I'm sorry, Ardi. Yin Yin is no longer suitable for this heroic prince. He is so handsome.'

Ardi laughed. 'Don't be sad. There are plenty of dolls like her in souvenir shops. In two months, I'll be there again. I'll find you a replacement, okay?'

The hint of a smile appeared on Grandma's lips. Yin Yin was removed from her dark drawer and placed on the chest alongside her new companion. Let her stay until her successor arrived – a new Yin Yin, more beautiful, unsullied.

Grandma and Grandpa would also get something new: happiness restored. Who knew exactly what form it would take, but it would feel warm and comfortable, hugging the body like a blanket and smelling as good as fresh baked bread.

The following day Sweetie disappeared. Nobody asked, nobody cared. A neighbour saw her roaming about, chased by strays and scavenging food from the trash.

Under the scorching sun Sweetie remembers her bowl. Grandma in the kitchen and Grandpa at the dining table. The old house where her tramp of a mother bore her and abandoned her. Yin Yin, the red-cheeked porcelain doll that shattered. All the memories remain in their designated place. Just as Yin Yin once stood securely on the antique chest.

If only Sweetie could speak, she would defend herself vigorously: yes, it's true that I toppled the porcelain doll. But how Yin Yin longed for her plunge. Sweetie saw everything, from the sweet little girl's eyes to her heart-shaped lips. Yin Yin was so lonely there, reduced to a flawless display, a source of pride. She didn't want to be a showpiece; she liked darkness and wanted to sleep with the devil. She wanted to kill herself.

And above all, she despised having her feet bound.

Apple and Knife

**'Do you want some, Eva?'**

For ten long seconds, she dangled the apple in front of me.

For ten long seconds, I gazed at her, the past roiling in my thoughts, the present refusing to vanish.

'Why that look on your face?' She giggled. 'I'm not going to poison you.'

I'd joined the design company a couple of months before, and my colleague had invited me over for a meal. Our chat about office politics had led to fond expressions of mutual support. When you grow up surrounded by vicious women, sisterhood becomes important.

But perhaps I was expecting something else.

The plump apple glistened, mouth-watering. Then she asked me if she looked like a witch. I observed her slender, damp fingers.

No wrinkles; no blue, bulging veins.

'I'll cut it for you,' she said.

She made the decision herself. She had no way of knowing that I couldn't look at an apple without thinking of Cousin Juli. Her ripe apples. Her glinting knife.

———

Cousin Juli was an attractive woman. She often wore a silk head-scarf that would slip down her sleek hair. My mother said she dyed it ever since grey streaks had begun to appear in its natural muted reddishness. Yet there was no denying that she was beautiful. Her round face was lit by a childlike glow. She applied pink lipstick to her pouty lips as delicately as she applied a matching blush. Her small eyes had full lashes, dark with mascara. She could have passed for a university student.

But Juli was no student. At that point, when I was seventeen, she was thirty-seven. She was the wife of Aziz, my oldest cousin. I had heard she was a promotions manager for a multinational automotive company. Her busy life meant she often got home late and couldn't attend our two types of major family gatherings: the arisan and Qur'anic recitations. I didn't know her that well, but she struck up conversation with me several times. She was the only relative who seemed eager to hear about my plans to major in design. My parents wanted me to study economics and work at a bank. In contrast, Cousin Juli encouraged my enthusiasm for design, telling me about all sorts of work opportunities. When she spoke, she put her broad knowledge on display and passion twinkled in her eyes. She moved in such an animated way. I was smitten with the lines at the corners of her eyes when she smiled. Smitten with her manicured fingers.

I don't know why Cousin Juli asked me about school so much. Perhaps she was staving off conversations with the older women. I know they peppered her with questions she didn't like. Family gatherings were an ordeal for her.

'Jul, when are you going to have another baby?' asked Aunt Romlah, my mother's older sister. 'The clock is ticking.'

'I'm still busy looking after Salwa,' she replied politely.

'Salwa's in primary school now. What are you so busy with? Give her a little brother or sister, so she doesn't get spoiled.'

'Aziz and I both work.'

'So quit, then. Aziz's business is thriving. What more do you need? You don't have to chase after money.'

Cousin Juli smiled. She did that whenever she didn't want to answer a question. She bowed her head like a well-behaved teenager being interrogated by her parents for coming home late.

Cousin Juli was a target for my relatives. She was sweet and enigmatic (or should I say that she was enigmatic because she was sweet?). They talked about her at recitations when she didn't show, debating whether she really could read Arabic script. She would only mumble incoherently when we all read the Sūrah Yā' Sīn of the Qur'an. If we held an arisan, she would always go home early instead of lingering to chat. 'She thinks she's too clever for us,' Aunt Yati concluded. My aunts commented on her reluctance to help in the kitchen. 'Look at her smooth fingers and those long, pink nails of hers. No housewife has fingers like that.' When she arrived at a wedding wearing a tight beige kebaya that left her shoulders bare, the gossip gathered momentum. Her hair was swept up in a high chignon and her long earrings grazed her sleek neck. Her skin was visible beneath a transparent brocade. 'See, Eva,' Cousin Aziz's younger sister, Rina, whispered in my ear. 'That's how married women use style to seduce men.'

People kept talking about her and she kept showing up at family gatherings often enough. In the eyes of my relatives, she remained a conundrum that refused to be simplified.

Then came the uproar. After talking for two hours on the phone with Aunt Yati, my mother delivered astonishing news: Cousin Juli was divorcing Aziz. Word had it that she was caught messing with a young boarder at their house. His name was Yusuf.

As the eldest son, Cousin Aziz had inherited his father's large home. Previously it belonged to my grandfather, a respected native Jakarta landowner. It consisted of seven rooms but, as usual for a mansion that had survived in the capital, its yard was so small as to look out of proportion with the house. The two rooms furthest from the family's private quarters were rented out to students or office workers. Yusuf had been there six months. He was twenty-three. After studying at a university in Padang, he had come to the capital in search of work. None of us had seen him in person yet, but we heard that he'd helped out with Cousin Aziz's vegetable distribution business and had even repaired a leak in their roof.

'It's a lesson, Eva,' my mother advised me. 'Don't let schooling ruin your morals.'

For over a month the phone rang off the hook. My aunts came to visit almost every day. They never let my mother know in advance but she inevitably welcomed them in. They would chatter in the living room while watching TV or at the table as they helped chop fruit and vegetables for the rujak. They had never been closer. Cousin Juli gave them a sense of shared destiny. They gossiped about her more freely at social gatherings and recitations because she never showed again.

'Shameful,' said Aunt Romlah. 'Aziz and Juli used to argue because Juli didn't want to rent out the room. And now look. She lures their boarder into her bed.'

'That's what happens when women are too smart,' chimed in Aunt Yati.

'That's what happens when women aren't religious,' Aunt Nur added.

'And with Aziz, she didn't even have to work. What more did she need?'

'Maybe she works so she can go on the prowl in her office. Remember that shiny lipstick and those lashes of hers?'

—

Sometimes it seemed like there was nothing new to talk about. It was the same old story, repeated over and over, all stitched together. But Cousin Juli was unquestionably magnetic; you couldn't ignore her. Perhaps what she did was wrong, but I didn't care. Other questions preoccupied me: what would she do now? Would I ever meet her again? Would she still wear pink lipstick and manicure her nails?

One day my mother fielded another bombshell of a call. Not from Aunt Romlah, Aunt Yati or another relative but from Cousin Juli herself. My mother's tone was friendly. I imagine that Cousin Juli's was no different. They asked after each other's news and then chatted about another cousin, who had just given birth. After their call Mum seemed dazed. She looked at me.

'Juli has invited us over next week.'

'An arisan?'

My mother shook her head.

'She said it's a silaturahmi.' She paused. 'A get-together to help patch up ties.'

'Will Cousin Aziz be there?'

'No, he moved out, but he's letting her stay in the house until the divorce is finalised. He's either too nice or just plain stupid.'

We thronged to her home for this gathering. It was strange that Cousin Juli had personally invited every single woman in our large family; all this time, it had seemed as if she was only pretending to get along with them.

'Did Juli not realise that we were talking about her relationship with that loafer?' Aunt Nur wondered aloud.

'Maybe not,' said Aunt Romlah. 'But it's never good to break ties. Anyway, aren't you all curious about young Yusuf? Whether he is living with her in the house? What he's like?'

The man was fourteen years her junior. For my aunts, there are thrills to be had in a visit to an enemy kingdom.

Contrary to our expectations, Cousin Juli welcomed us with great warmth. She was wearing a purple dress tailored to hug the curves of her body. There were strands of greying hair at her temples. She was as beautiful as ever. Dishes were served buffet style on a long table. Some aunts were clustered in fixed spots, sitting in chairs or cross-legged on mats, doing their best to avoid conversation with the hostess. The prevailing attitude among them seemed to be: let the old ladies deal with her; we're only rookies. But Cousin Juli came over to each of us by turn. The house became a chessboard that pitted the guests against Cousin Juli. My aunts had to search for things to talk about, to deftly thrust and parry.

'Maybe this is the last time we'll see each other,' said Cousin Juli when she approached our group: Mother, Aunt Romlah, Cousin Rina, and me. I noticed the selection on her plate. Rice, coconut chicken, beef liver in sambal.

Talk died down, and I saw Mother and Aunt Romlah exchange sidelong glances. For a while, nobody mentioned the divorce. Finally, Aunt Romlah spoke up: 'Don't let the ties between us be broken, Jul. We'll always be family.'

Cousin Juli's lips curled into a smile, and those endearing wrinkles appeared at the corners of her eyes.

The conversation moved on from the cousin who had given birth to the plans the mothers had for their children's schooling. No one raised the issue of the divorce or Cousin Juli's infidelity. Then two maids brought out dessert. Each guest was given a small plate containing a red apple and a sharpened knife. Something odd was going on.

Cousin Juli apologised for the inelegant dessert. She had wanted to make a chocolate cream pie but her cholesterol was becoming a concern. Doctor's orders.

'Surely not. You aren't the least bit fat,' said Cousin Rina. 'Anyway, apples are fine.'

'Apples truly are tasty,' Cousin Juli murmured, fondling one. She picked up a knife and began to peel.

The women around her exchanged glances but out of respect for their hostess they also took up their knives and sliced into their own apples. As the youngest in the room, I waited for my elders until I realised I had no desire for fresh fruit. I noticed Cousin Juli whisper something to her maid. The young girl nodded and left the room.

I studied the apple in Cousin Juli's hands. The section turned towards me, yet to be peeled, was red, round and ripe. The sharp blade was so shiny I could see a reflection. Was that my face? No, it was hers. Something crept into the gleaming corners of her eyes and loomed in the furrows that appeared in her forehead when she smiled. That smile highlighted her sweet, ageing lines and revealed her uneven teeth. Her childlike teeth, the canines too long.

As the women were busy slicing their apples, Cousin Juli said, 'Let me introduce you to Yusuf.'

Her voice sounded so calm.

All heads turned towards a figure entering the dining room. He was taking careful steps. In this room of middle-aged matrons his youth shimmered. He was tall, his shoulders were straight, and his arms were sturdy. He wore a short-sleeved shirt that showed off his gleaming, chocolate flesh. His eyebrows were as jet black as his piercing eyes. For me, he was not so different from boys my age who were idolised by girls. He was simple but he radiated childlike appeal. His wild, curly hair, his strong cheekbones and his full lips all invited caressing.

Yusuf.

Time stopped. The women held their breath, staring at the young man. They didn't blink; their hands clutched their knives. Faint sounds escaped their lips. Agonised groans as their fingers continued peeling. The tough skin of apples that had passed the point of ripeness. Were they even apples? I caught another scent. An ancient, intoxicating aroma. Blood flowed from my aunts' palms, slicking the knives, coating the apples, staining the table-cloths. Chunks of apples were cast to the floor. Drops of fresh blood seeped out and darkened. Cousin Juli's knives had been readied, but not to pierce the flesh of apples.

Yusuf bowed, pale. He was like a trembling angel, his wings rent by the penetrating gaze of the women, who were carried away in a frenzy. Soon he fell. Like Maenads, they crowded around him. Cousin Juli looked upon her victims, still under the spell of their own passion, a passion that had stolen in amid the blood and pain. Eventually everything blurred; it was no longer clear who was victim, who was tormentor, who enjoyed pleasure, who suffered pain. They scratched deeper and deeper at their lust. The women had come together in Cousin Juli's web, enveloped in an aroma of meat and fruit, so fresh. She gave a winsome smile.

She glanced at the chocolate angel, then her eyes turned towards me. I felt fragile and soon fell.

*Your wings are torn, let me patch them. Like the way I patch my ties with others.*

Slowly, so slowly, Juli licked her lips.

———

'Ouch!' She had hurt herself, cutting the apple carelessly. Was this involuntary manslaughter, or a premeditated act? My apple. I approached her.

'Does it hurt?'

She closed her eyes, not answering.

'Let me see.'

She held out a bleeding hand. I took hold of her long, tapering fingers. They brought back memories of Cousin Juli. Succulent, smooth, nails painted pink. We stood so close, this apple cutter and I. Her fringe fell on her forehead, strand by strand leading fingers astray.

My breathing gets rough when I see the colour red. A fragrance, so intimate, tickled my nose. It reminded me of beginnings. My mouth watered, but not because of the apple.

Slowly, so slowly, I licked the wound on her finger.

**The cold-blooded killer puts down the book she is reading.**
A thousand fireflies in Manhattan? It's all very well to write about
home from far away, but she doesn't share her compatriot's nos-
talgic sentiments. After all, she is a cold-blooded killer. So she
launches her own plot starring a woman who dies without ever
seeing a single firefly.

From her own far-off location in space and time, the killer
spies Epon and her strange habits. Yes. At the stroke of midnight,
while her husband slumbers, Epon will leave her house and head
to the cemetery to see the firefly, for Epon believes this firefly –
a shimmering female, who transforms herself to attract the male,
only to prey upon him later – appears nowhere else. Of course,
Toha, her husband, will grow agitated. In the peaceful, tight-knit
village of Cibeurit, women do not roam about in the dark and

especially don't visit the cemetery. His wife could be thought
a devotee of black magic.

A few nights before the sad event, Toha will ambush Epon as
she is tiptoeing out of the room.

'Where are you going? Why are you creeping around like
a mouse?'

Epon, heavily pregnant, will return to bed without seeing the
firefly.

At the end of her life Epon will have never seen a real firefly.
But a tiny baby will be born into the arms of Aunt Icih, a healer
and midwife. The baby will be a girl, lovely, as if gifted with gleaming wings. A beautiful firefly, Epon will murmur before she dies.

Our killer agrees, although she also has her eye on a firefly in
another graveyard.

—

The cold-blooded killer is still skulking around Cibeurit, even
though it remains indistinct and fragmented. She knows that
Toha named his daughter Maimunah. Although nothing connected Maimunah with fireflies, the villagers agreed that she glowed.

At thirteen, Maimunah attracted the young men of Cibeurit.
Yet many were reluctant to approach her because she was too tall,
or at least taller than average for girls of the village. Her childhood
friends nicknamed her Longlegs. The unmarried youth felt inferior
before her, worried about being ridiculed as midgets by jealous
rivals. They also worried when picturing Maimunah ten years
hence, remembering that the girls of Cibeurit tended to plump
up after marriage and their first child. After passing her prime,
Maimunah would be a large, tall woman, a giantess. Even now
she was quite imposing.

Feeling no different from other women, Maimunah walked upright, back straight and chest out. Her long, curly hair danced to the swaying of her hips. She never held back her opinions. Toha began to fret because his daughter feared nothing. With her provocative walk, she could be raped by goons on her way home from bathing in the river. Now, in this peaceful village none of the lads were hooligans. But chaos could arrive with transients, like the gangs of criminals who wandered from forest to forest stealing, violating innocent girls and then vanishing. The sight of Maimunah's wet tresses would surely make them lick their chops. And it was the end of the story for a girl if she lost her virginity.

At seventeen, Maimunah grew tired of being the centre of attention. She welcomed her admirers but soon grew bored with them in turn. They didn't want to know anything about a woman beyond what was to be found inside her bra. Maimunah preferred to spend her time at the house of Aunt Icih. In her eyes, Aunt Icih possessed extraordinary knowledge. Every day she grappled with spread legs, the darkness of the womb, and clots of blood beneath women's sarongs. Women living; women dying. From the shaman, Maimunah came to know how her mother had looked before death snatched her away.

'Your mother said you're beautiful like a firefly.'

'Where can I see a firefly?'

'I've never seen one myself, but your mother said a firefly dances in the graveyard.'

History repeated itself. Like Epon, Maimunah went to seek that sparkling creature. However, it was not a firefly that she met but Jaja, the cemetery watchman. He rarely showed himself as he was often mocked. He was a dwarf, only reaching Maimunah's waist, dark-skinned and bald with a bristly moustache. Hair covered his stubby hands. The movements of his tiny body were so nimble that the village children dubbed him a giant rat. King Rat. The adults forbade their children to make fun of others because that was not the nature of the people of Cibeurit, but none of them were eager to linger with the watchman.

The first time he encountered Maimunah, Jaja simply looked up for a moment from the grave he was digging. He enjoyed his work so much that saliva would collect at the edges of his perpetually open mouth.

'If you become a corpse, you will be just as ugly as me,' Jaja said, wiping the spittle at the corner of his lips.

Perhaps because radiance didn't dazzle Jaja, in the eyes of Maimunah he was more interesting than the youths of Cibeurit. Rotting meat fascinated the man more than fresh meat. While Aunt Icih held the secret of life behind the stained red of women's sarongs, Jaja knew of all that was destroyed, decayed and porous. He possessed the key to the world of the dead.

Toha began to get wind of Maimunah's odd relationship with the graveyard, like her mother before her. His face went white when a few people reported Maimunah's intimacy with the watchman. That couldn't be allowed. It was time to act decisively on behalf of his beloved daughter's future. Toha offered Maimunah in marriage to Suparna, the village head, as his second wife. In his forties, Suparna owned acres of rice paddies and a jeep. Suparna understood Toha's anxiety and, as befitting a resident of Cibeurit, prepared to come to the aid of a neighbour in need, he opened his arms wide to rescue Maimunah's honour.

The day before her marriage to Suparna, Maimunah approached Jaja and looked at him with a bitter expression on her face.

'Take me away,' she whispered.

Jaja knew he would never be able to make Maimunah happy and so he murmured, 'I only take away the dead.'

For the sake of the peace of the village, the young girl married. She lived in a house big enough to hold both her and Euis, Suparna's first wife. Each week, Suparna spent three nights with Maimunah, while the remainder belonged to Euis. Maimunah helped Euis care for her three children in accordance with the traditional co-operation of Cibeurit women.

The killer is still keeping watch, refining her plot, sipping her drink. A killer's instinct always ferrets out the openings that lead into any shelter. She smiles, well aware that when Maimunah was not with Suparna she met Jaja at the cemetery.

Maimunah went out at night, even when pregnant. The villagers caught whiff of her dark affair with the dwarf watchman. Several people claimed to have seen a tall woman and a dwarf entangled in the bushes. The residents of Cibeurit were not prone to gossip, but acts of abomination needed to be dealt with. When Maimunah gave birth to a baby boy, the uproar was inevitable. Aunt Icih, the healer midwife, offered her praise: 'Handsome.'

But the baby was not handsome. Its body was small, hairy, almost rat-like. The rumours of Maimunah's affair must have been true. Damn it to hell! Suparna punched the wall until his knuckles bled. He gave his wife, the sinner, one night to prepare to leave his home. How shameful to have a baby that resembled a rodent. A bastard child, no doubt!

The next day, the whole house was awakened by Euis's screams. She met with a plague of rats pouring forth from her husband's room – he had been spending one last night with Maimunah. Hordes of black, slimy animals passed between her legs. Hundreds, maybe even a thousand of them, running amok. Maimunah was nowhere to be found. Only Suparna was dead, in horrific fashion.

His flesh had been shredded, as if it had been gnawed throughout the night. Blood and tufts of fur covered the ulcerations that were his eyes. The rats scurried about.

The predatory rodents quickly spread throughout the village into the wells, the jars, the stores of rice. The inhabitants of Cibeurit had no opportunity to grieve for their village head as, in no time at all, the close-knit, peaceful community was attacked by plague. Corpses lay stretched out at every corner. No one was buried because Jaja had suddenly vanished as if sucked up in putrid air and a puddle of vomit. The village of Cibeurit was hemmed in by the stench of rats. The stench of disease, of death.

The long-legged woman and her dwarf lover were never found. The villagers believe Maimunah had gone off with King Rat and cursed the village. Those who escaped death formed a pact to forget and wandered like a gang of rogues. The kinship ties of Cibeurit dissolved. Aunt Icih, one of the survivors, told this tale to pregnant mothers who came to her. Destiny's decree allowed her to live and to become the holder of a secret, though she was never able to answer the question of the mothers who asked:

'Who sent those man-eating rats?'

—

May, the cold-blooded killer, has satisfied her appetite for destruction. She closes her small notebook. Yes. Satisfied. Her story is complete.

She parts her long curly hair, which dances to the swaying of her hips. Her eyes fix on the large crystal globe hanging from the ceiling, glowing like a planet in the evening sky. A writer who favours nostalgia over murder would certainly interpret this sparkling as a kind of firefly.

The woman doesn't think she will put the finishing touches on her story in this Chinatown nightclub. She sips her drink again. Like many women of Manhattan, she is devoted to Cosmopolitans. Vodka, Cointreau, lemon, cranberry. She has always seen herself as a cocktail hotchpotch. Gado-gado is a hotchpotch too, but gado-gado signifies home, a native village, a longed-for place. It doesn't mean journey.

On its journey, a pack of criminals murders and leaves a trail. When a foot gets entangled, it's not easy to search for a shoe that has been tossed who knows where. May knows that one shoe was left in the village Cibeurit, so she finishes off that close-knit, peaceful village before it destroys her. She kills off the place and the memories lovingly, as if killing the father. In New York City, with a single shoe, she survives, like the thieves. Summon up the places of your past, then destroy them! Distant places, indistinct, remembered in fragments.

May's intention to leave the nightclub is stayed by a sparkling figure. A firefly? Near her table sits a thickly moustachioed man in a gold robe. A sparkling cap covers his head. May squints, trying to convince herself she isn't drunk. The man is no stranger. How short his legs are: dangling, not reaching the floor. May shudders, struck by a flash of realisation.

The dwarf watchman. He makes an appearance in this city, not a butt of jokes as in Cibeurit but a petty rajah. King Rat. May observes the staff in his hand. A crystal globe sits on its tip. It looks like a miniature disco ball.

May's heart pounds. She thinks that Cibeurit has been obliterated, but its characters live on, forcing their way into her place of refuge. They have found her out. Cleverly, he has disguised himself as a fortune-teller. Though a little afraid, May wants to approach him to ask a question – or more accurately, to demand an answer, as when Maimunah whispered to her lover, 'Tell me what the future holds.'

But the dwarf remains motionless, preoccupied with a martini, and doesn't even glance in her direction. May gives the shirt that he is wearing a once-over. The words 'Little Johnny' are emblazoned across it. She comes crashing to earth.

She finishes her drink, laughing at herself for believing that the uneffaced remnants of Cibeurit have suddenly appeared in a Manhattan club. What a fool. He is Johnny, not Jaja. Swallowing back her disappointment, either because she feels stupid or because Jaja apparently is Johnny, May turns her attention to the crowd on the dance floor. The clubbers cheer when the DJ they've been waiting for mounts the stage. The music throbs like the raucous cries of thousands of famished rats. The club goers pump their arms in the air, entrusting their happiness to the skilled hands of the DJ.

The man next to May disappears. Now Little Johnny is on stage, beside the DJ, dancing with an extremely tall blonde. May takes a breath, feeling a second slap. The dwarf and the long-legged woman are part of tonight's show.

Perhaps Longlegs is the dwarf's lover. For some reason May is jealous, wondering why she is always the odd one out in a ménage à trois.

At that moment May understands that she is a firefly swirling like a disco light. It's time to go. She weaves through the crowd of dancers, looking for the exit. She passes the club's bouncer; some people are still queuing up to see the DJ. She wants to run, to rush, to damn the firefly, to await the attack of plague that obliterates all.

But she is a cold-blooded killer, and she is haunted.

On the Chinatown sidewalk, now growing quiet at one in the morning, something stays her steps. Not a firefly but Little Johnny standing before her, wiping away spittle at the corner of his lips.

The dwarf who only takes away the dead.

In front of the man with his bristly moustache, May stands like a statue. She cannot believe what she hears.

*Where have all the rats gone?*

## Author's acknowledgements

—

I would like to thank Stephen J Epstein for his faith,
persistence, and creativity in translating my short stories.
It was a great pleasure to work with Stephen, and also with
Brow Books, one of the most fearless and cutting-edge
independent literary platforms in Australia. Many thanks to
Elizabeth Bryer, Sam Cooney and Dzenana Vucic for their
insightful comments and suggestions that helped me see my
work with a fresh eye, and thanks to Brett Weekes and
Rosetta Mills for their work on the Australian edition of
*Apple and Knife*.

The UK edition of the book would not have been
possible without the commitment and enthusiasm of
editor Ellie Steel and her team at Harvill Secker.
I am indebted to them and to my agent, Kelly Falconer,
for her guidance and encouragement.

I highly appreciate the assistance from the LitRI Translation
Grant as well as generous support from friends and
institutions: Tiffany Tsao, John McGlynn (Lontar Foundation),
Mirna Yulistianti (Gramedia Pustaka Utama), and the
Department of Media, Music, Communication and Cultural
Studies at Macquarie University.

I would like to thank my parents – especially my mother, the first disobedient woman who inspired many of my early stories. Finally, I dedicate this book to both my partner/collaborator/first reader, Ugoran Prasad, and my daughter, Ilana, who have travelled and crossed many borders with me in the past decade.

## Translator's acknowledgements

Participation in this project has been a highlight of my academic and translating career, and I need to thank several people who have helped bring it to fruition. I would like to thank John McGlynn of the Lontar Foundation, who has been a great supporter of my forays into translating Indonesian fiction, and first introduced me to the work of Intan Paramaditha. Tiffany Tsao offered wonderful editing suggestions and played a key role in connecting us to TLB/ Brow Books, who have been terrific to work with as publishers. Many thanks to TLB's Sam Cooney, Elizabeth Bryer and Dzenana Vucic for their infectious enthusiasm and thoughtful reading of the stories, which has led to significant improvements. Sora Kim-Russell also read several of the stories, and her sharp translator's eye has made for a better collection. I also want to acknowledge my many fine colleagues at Victoria University of Wellington and the New Zealand Centre for Literary Translation; it's great to have such a congenial work environment.